OLIV
DULCINITES

by

GEOFFREY ALLEN

CHIMERA

Olivia and the Dulcinites first published in 1997 by
Chimera Publishing Ltd
PO Box 152
Waterlooville
Hants
PO8 9FS

Printed and bound in Great Britain by
Caledonian International Book Manufacturing Ltd Glasgow

New authors welcome

OLIVIA AND THE DULCINITES

Geoffrey Allen

This novel is fiction - in real life practice safe sex

FOREWORD

This novel is primarily a work of fiction, but to an extent has been drawn from factual accounts recorded by those who actually witnessed the tortures and trials of the Middle Ages, and the period leading up to the end of the 17th Century. Both the wheel and the rack were common instruments of torture used extensively to extract confessions or instil terror in those insubordinate to both Church and State.

The use of hallucinogenic drugs was reputedly employed at witches' sabbaths and ceremonies throughout the Middle Ages. It has been suggested that many of the visions and revelations seen and recorded by those who experienced them in the 14th and 15th Centuries may have been inspired from the use of rotting grain in the baking of bread. The grain would be stored from a successful harvest and carried over in case of failure the following year. The fermenting grain produced a chemical not dissimilar to that used in the production of LSD, and it may not be too fanciful to suggest that the fantastic images conjured by mediaeval artists and described in this novel may have been drug induced.

Without doubt, learned men and women practising medicine at that time were all too well aware of the enormous power that lay at their disposal, hence the importance played by the herbalist in the convent of Saint Dulcinea.

The rest is fiction.

Geoffrey Allen. March 1997.

PROLOGUE

April 1442

It was in early spring that the Holy Inquisition was despatched to the convent of Saint Dulcinea. More than forty men-at-arms toiled up the steep track that led to the convent walls. Only with great difficulty could the waggon follow at their rear. As they drew nearer a strange sound came from the waggon to the windows above; a sound not unlike the clattering of cutlery or the rattling of chains.

"What do they want with us?" asked a pretty nun of not more than twenty summers. She stood beside the Abbess, a woman ten or fifteen years her senior. Both watched the men below preparing to batter down the great oak door.

"They have come to punish us," the Abbess replied grimly. "And to turn us out of our convent."

The throat of the young nun contracted with fear. "But why would they punish us? And why - ?"

"Because we are Dulcinites. Because we believe in and worship the pleasures of the flesh."

Both women were naked, and had just risen from the bed they had been sharing. The crumpled and damp sheets bore witness to a session of relentless and passionate lovemaking.

And so it was throughout the convent; nuns rising from shared beds and listening in wonderment and trepidation to the hollow, mournful booming of the battering-ram, which soon climaxed with a sharp cracking of splintering wood.

The men-at-arms streamed through the shattered door and into the quadrangle. Behind them followed the waggon. The Abbess knew what it contained.

Some of the convent's plate and coin had been deliberately left for the Inquisition. But the greater part, along with the sacred books, had been hidden in a cart and covered with the carcass of a rotting sheep. The stench would keep the men-at-arms away - the Abbess hoped.

"Are those the instruments of our punishment?" the young nun asked.

The Abbess nodded gravely as the waggon was unloaded and the instruments carried down the steps that led to the crypt. She looked down upon the nuns who were assembling timidly in the quadrangle. Many had not even the time to dress properly and stood shivering in their shifts. Those foolish enough to take refuge in their cells were quickly discovered and dragged screaming to join their companions.

The Abbess turned the young nun towards her and they kissed tenderly. Outside in the corridor the vile curses and heavy tramp of booted feet drew nearer. The fingers of the Abbess dug deep into the firmly clenched buttocks of her lover. "They are coming for us," she whispered, and then pulled away.

The young nun snatched up her habit and threw it over her head. The Abbess covered herself with a blanket and together they made their way to the quadrangle. Already the nuns were filing down the steps of the crypt.

Robert of Gaunt, the Inquisitor, ordered the nuns to gather at the far end of the room where they could watch the instruments of punishment being assembled. He had chosen wisely, for the crypt was devoid of any windows and lighted with nothing more luminous than a few guttering candles. In the half-light and eerie silence, broken only by hammering and nailing, the construction of the instruments took shape. Filled with curious horror the nuns clutched each other as a huge wooden frame was erected. It was a giant 'T', standing about eight feet tall. The crossbar, fitted with chains and rings at each end, was not fixed rigidly to the top of the vertical, but was able to rotate a full turn.

When the hammering and nailing had ceased the Inquisitor approached the Abbess. Without speaking he gripped the blanket and ripped it from her shoulders. She was tall for a woman, taller than the Inquisitor, even in bare feet. The hair at her fork glistened with a velvet sheen, a perfect triangle that followed the crease of her thighs and settled under the pit of her stomach in a gorgeous concave.

"I have no desire to harm you," he said, standing so close her nipples almost touched his armoured chest. "Indeed, you can put an end to these torments before they even begin. Open your heart and tell me the whereabouts of your plate, and I will consider this trial over. Then you can all go your way in peace."

"I shall not tell you."

A step nearer and her nipples stiffened against his cold armour. Then in a loud voice that brooked no argument he commanded the nuns to strip naked. Gasps of horror escaped their lips. It was unheard of that a nun should strip in front of a man - let alone men. They tugged their habits tighter about them. Those who had not the time to put on their habits and were clothed only in their under-garments hid themselves further into the gloom.

"Is it necessary that my Sisters take off their clothes?" asked the Abbess firmly.

"Very necessary," he assured her. "Do you think I intend to flog them through all that cloth? A woman is much better served for a whip on her bare hinds."

The nuns looked at him beseechingly, but he was adamant. Any argument was futile.

Slowly and with trembling fingers they began to disrobe. Mindful that the greedy eyes of the soldiers were watching their every move, they first removed their head-dresses and then, more reluctantly, the cumbersome habits. Stripped down to their shifts they made one last appeal for clemency. But none came. It was all part of the procedure that those facing interrogation should be naked, for in that state they would feel utterly vulnerable and defenceless; less likely to resist and more likely to cooperate. They raised their shifts an inch at a time, gathering them in folds at the knees. Shapely white legs gradually revealed themselves, and then bellies and breasts, until each and every girl stood as required.

For some considerable time the men-at-arms marveled at the nuns' youth and beauty. Some were tall and long legged. Others were shorter but no less shapely. Some were pert breasted, others much more full. It was not surprising that under the lustful glare of the men they each hung their heads in shame.

Not so the Abbess, who stood with her head held high. Resigned to her fate she remained perfectly composed. The Inquisitor again asked the whereabouts of the plate. Again she refused.

"Very well. You leave me little choice but to make use of the instruments."

"I am not frightened of that," she replied bravely.

A wolfish grin spread across his lean face. "You may not be frightened, but your Sisters are. See how they huddle together like sheep."

There was no denying that. At the mere mention of the contraptions the nuns had closed together, more fearful of impending punishment than their own nakedness. Many had broken into a cold sweat which trickled in rivulets between their breasts and over their bellies and into the fringes of their pubic hair. The youngest, the lover of the Abbess, had wet herself, and stood paralysed in the puddle forming at her feet.

"You will select two of your Sisters as an example to the rest, and also as proof of my sincerity and your disobedience. Now choose."

A terrible wailing and sobbing arose. The Abbess remained silent.

"If you do not make your choice immediately I shall have them all whipped," he added flatly.

It was not an easy choice for the Abbess to make, for none of the Sisters knew where the plate and coin were hidden. She had to decide whether seeing her Sisters cruelly flogged was worth her silence. The small amount set by would remain hidden until she judged the punishment severe enough to loosen her tongue. If she surrendered too readily it would arouse the Inquisitor's suspicions. There was no alternative but to subject her Sisters to the whip. "Sister Ruth and Sister Catherine."

The chosen nuns stepped timidly from the darkened huddle and into the candlelight. They were amongst the tallest of the assembly, of equal height, build and weight. The Abbess had chosen them because their voluptuous bodies could withstand the severest of beatings.

"Before they are whipped I am required by law to carry out an inspection. A mere formality, but one with which I must comply."

So saying, the Inquisitor stepped forward. The envy on the faces of his men could not be disguised as he closed his hand around the breasts of the dark-haired girl. He squeezed gently at first, as he might with a lover or nervous virgin, thumbing her nipples and gently increasing the pressure. Then, much to the horror of all and sundry he bent his head to the cupped breast and bit the aroused nipple. Catherine grit her teeth, but refused to cry out.

"You have been trained well," he complimented. He lightly patted her bare bottom, the strength increasing until hard slaps reverberated around the dingy cellar. She visibly winced, but remained silent. "A pair of firm buttocks," he observed. "I wonder if your legs are as well constructed."

He slapped her flanks and hams, progressing steadily down her thighs and paying great attention to the insides where experience had taught him women were at their most sensitive. He was not disappointed, for the gritted teeth parted and she uttered a low moan. The moan became a harsh grunt as his hand strayed to her pudenda, the fingers slipping deftly inside her parted slit.

"As I thought," he announced coldly. "The girl is wet."

The nuns watched with abject terror as he fingered her, worming his hand deep into her groin, his wrist blatantly twisting back and forth. When his hand was withdrawn, soaked with her juice, he used it to slap the backs of her knees and calves, returning to her hips, belly, and lastly her breasts. He struck left and right, making the orbs swing and dance and all the while arousing her nipples to greater erection.

"The sargeant may have the honour of inspecting the other," he said, indicating Ruth.

She was not of such strong mettle as her companion, and when the sargeant came forward her hands flew to cover the join of her thighs, as well they might. He advanced upon her with three long strides. The lust in his eyes alone made her tremble.

"Take your hands away from there," he rasped, and before the poor girl could comply he slapped her forearms.

"Put your hands on your head - and keep them there!"

He was built like an ox, and beneath the stubble on his chin ran a deep, livid scar; a knife wound. The eyes were grey and cruel. He grabbed her breasts with both hands and squeezed until tears flowed down her cheeks. The nipples he pinched and twisted, his teeth crushed the teats amid sobs of pain. Neither were his slaps gentle. The flat of his hands hit over her ribcage and hips. Her bottom blazed red, as did the tops of her thighs. She was crying and shaking her head, but he was relentless. He slapped her bottom with the full strength of his hand, making her jolt forward in agony. As a finale he attempted to repeat the actions of his master by inserting a finger inside her, but to his chagrin was ordered away.

"The girl has been satisfactorily examined," said the Inquisitor in a rare fit of leniency. "Now take them both to the frame."

The two chosen nuns were positioned beneath and at either end of the crossbar. They stood to attention as instructed, with their arms by their sides and legs firmly together. Beautiful in their symmetry, they watched breathlessly as the men-at-arms took up the candelabrum and brought them close, illuminating their naked bodies.

Catherine was ordered to place her hands in front of her while a pair of shackles were fetched. These were fitted around her wrists, and when the attending soldier was satisfied that they were tightly secured and there was no possibility of her hands sliding free, he fastened a length of chain to them. He then reached up and passed the chain through the ring at the end of the crossbar, and left the loose end to dangle down to her waist.

When satisfied, he moved to Ruth, who dutifully placed her hands at her front. Her nipples, breasts and bottom were still smarting from the bites and slaps of the sargeant, and in the candlelight took on a reddish golden hue.

"Lie on the floor," the Inquisitor instructed. "On your back with your knees drawn to your chest."

Although obviously baffled, she obeyed, lying directly beneath the end of the crossbar, her knees drawn up and resting on her breasts. Another man-at-arms knelt at her bottom, and with the same precision as his comrade he produced a pair of iron shackles and locked them tightly around her ankles. A similar length of chain was fastened to them, and passed up and through the ring at the opposite end of the wooden span. This was then left dangling like the first.

Leaving the nuns for a moment, the Inquisitor ordered the sargeant to bring forward the modes of punishment. He took one of them and listened with a triumphant sneer to the gasps of horror coming from the naked assembly who were now herded closer to the frame. The whip was not a single length of leather, but half a dozen strips knotted in their middle and at their ends. Carefully, almost lovingly, he passed the knotted ends over the belly of the nun prostrated on the flagstones. The same light touch was applied to her standing companion, the knotted ends draped over her shoulders so that they touched upon her nipples.

"This is for you," the Inquisitor whispered, loud enough for all to hear.

While Catherine stood openmouthed in terror, he displayed the other mode of punishment; a rod, which he flicked over the nipples of the prostrated Ruth. The rod was in fact a plaited leather cord, but so thick it took on the appearance of a cane or stout stick. At its end it tapered to a strand no thicker than the little finger of a child.

"And now we are ready to begin," he announced.

A man-at-arms stepped from the shadows and took hold of the chain that hung behind Catherine. It rattled through the ring in the crossbar, and her arms slowly lifted until they stretched as if she were reaching for the ceiling. She squealed when, with a sudden tug, she was up on tiptoe. Another rattle of the links lifted her toes just clear of the floor. While she hung there - every muscle in her legs, torso and arms straining from the weight - the chain was fastened around the crossbar.

"Now the other," ordered the Inquisitor.

The same procedure was followed, except that Ruth was hauled up by her ankles until her head hovered an inch or so over the flags. Her arms flopped down onto the floor, but were quickly gathered, pinioned behind her back, and fastened at the wrist with iron cuffs. A perfect balance had been achieved at either end of the crossbar; a pair of scales equally weighted.

The Inquisitor turned to face the Abbess. With the rod he struck her flanks. It was not a severe blow, but hard enough to leave a mark and make her cry out.

"I shall give you one last chance to reveal the whereabouts of your gold. You will answer directly, and if it is brought before me without delay not a single blow shall be struck. I promise you of that. Now speak!"

The Abbess stared past him at the frame. The naked bodies of her Sisters glowed in the candlelight. Their flesh glistened with sweat. Their faces were masks of anguish. For a moment it seemed as if she would break, but with dogged determination she shook her head and turned away.

The Inquisitor sighed. "As you wish, Reverend Mother." He handed the whip to the sargeant and tossed the rod to the nearest man-at-arms. The nuns hanging from the frame would now be flogged, and in so doing the true purpose of the frame would at last be revealed.

The sargeant, being superior in rank to the soldier, was the first to strike. He stood behind Catherine and a little to the left. He did not hit her at once but hesitated, getting the measure of the heavy whip; its length and weight; where he intended to strike first; which part of her body would cause her the greatest suffering.

The Abbess stared at the Inquisitor with glazed hatred. At a barely perceptible nod of his menacing head the whip whistled through the heavy air.

The crack of leather on flesh was like a bolt of lightning. The thongs spread upon impact, catching Catherine square across her buttocks, covering every inch of the cheeks. Gritting her teeth, she steeled herself against the searing pain, determined to resist. Her body tensed, the muscles turned to iron, and when the next blow fell viciously across her back she screamed and jolted forwards. The multitudinous shock of the thongs sent her legs flaying. Propelled by her writhing weight the crossbar started to move, and as it did so the rod fell on the buttocks of Ruth with the same force as the whip that had landed on Catherine.

If Catherine had screamed, Ruth howled like one demented; a high pitched howl which pierced the ears of the watching nuns. So frantic were her attempts to avoid the next blow she twisted and turned by the ankles.

"Her thighs, strike her thighs!"

The soldier obeyed his commander, as at the same time the whip fell on the backs of Catherine's knees. Both women broke into a desperate writhing, far greater than before. Their thrashing legs and hips sent the crossbar furiously squeaking around, and when it halted it was to position Ruth for the whip and Catherine for the rod. Thus they would both feel the wrath of each tormenting weapon.

Catherine was brave and proud; but her resistance was short-lived. The heavy plaited leather landed with a smack across her full breasts, the aim delivered so perfectly that each nipple was crushed under its stinging weight. She held her breath until the next blow cut into her stretched belly. The air rushed from her lungs and she too span on her chain.

The whip caught Ruth on her buttocks, and with such violence she almost bent double. Her back arched, lifting her head away from the floor. Her body was sent swinging crazily through the air, and the crossbar repeated its terrible journey. It creaked to a stop and both women were now back where they had started.

The flogging stopped for a moment while the Inquisitor offered the Abbess another chance to put an end to their sufferings. She refused, judging he would be suspicious of such a hasty capitulation.

It mattered not to the Inquisitor. Time was on his side. If neccssary he would have the women flogged raw.

"Lay on the lashes slowly," he said to the soldiers. "If the Abbess is so sure that her Sisters can take it I want them to feel every lash. Whip the bitches senseless."

The soldiers shrugged as if to say it was all the same to them. From that moment on each blow was carefully aimed to inflict the maximum of pain. They took their time, prolonging the punishment. They paused for rest and refreshed themselves from flagons of wine, while the poor nuns were left hanging by their chains.

As the punishment continued those men who remained idle sidled up to the gathered nuns and steered them to the darkest corners of the crypt. The outnumbered nuns had little choice but to comply; the sight of their whipped sisters made them fearful to resist.

Despite instinctive pleas for mercy, they were taken in a variety of positions, the favourite and the one which offered the easiest of access to their groins was to bend them over the wine barrels.

Neither did the men spare mouths or bottom-holes. Now that all control was lost it seemed anything was fair game.

The Abbess, powerless to prevent what was in effect the wholesale violation of her convent, sat on a step with her head in her hands. She was unaware of the men behind her. A hand lighted on each shoulder, and she looked up into the face of the Inquisitor. There was no anger in his countenance, just an expression of tired impatience. Behind him hung the exhausted Catherine and Ruth.

"They took their punishment well," he conceded. "I wonder if the rest of your Sisters will display as much courage."

The Abbess stared up into his heartless eyes. "You mean to flog the remainder of my Sisters?"

"I shall have the whole convent flogged unless you tell me what I want to know."

She looked down at the dusty flagstones. "The plate is in the well."

"You see. You could tell me after all. What a pity you did not do so earlier. It would have saved you so much anguish, not to mention the sufferings of your Sisters." He waved a hand and a soldier immediately disappeared to find the well and the hidden treasure.

Catherine and Ruth were taken down from the cruel apparatus. They had fainted and lay supine on the flagstones, their breasts heaving as if in heavy slumber. The Abbess would have gone to them, but the men whose hands still rested on her shoulders forbade her to move.

When the soldier returned with the plate the Inquisitor seemed satisfied.

"Will you let us be now?" asked the Abbess.

"But of course - after you have fulfilled your duty."

"My duty? Have I not given you what you wanted? And have my Sisters not suffered in the process?"

"Indeed. Now it is only you who remains to be punished."

"Me? Why me?"

"Because you have been disobedient, and because you have put me to a great deal of unnecessary trouble."

The Abbess looked at the frame. "You're going to whip me."

"Not necessarily. It all depends on how cooperative you are."

"But, I have given you everything."

The Inquisitor chuckled. "Not quite."

A look of terrible realization crept across her face. "Surely, you don't mean ..."

He was already unbuckling his breeches. The armour would be too much trouble to take off, and besides, he wanted to be back in the town before nightfall. "Kindly bend over that barrel," he said.

She looked to the barrel he indicated. The two soldiers guided her to it. A long sigh escaped her lips and slowly, without any emotion, she lowered herself over the wood as though about to be beheaded. Someone grabbed her ankles and pulled them over the flags, not stopping until her legs were stretched fully open.

The Inquisitor, with his perverse sense of humour and love of irony, ordered two of the nuns to come forward. "You may have the honour of holding your Reverend Mother still while I give her what she should have had in the first place," he remarked drily.

The barrel was perfect for the taking of a woman. Its natural shape enabled it to rock steadily back and forth while he penetrated her, the nuns holding her shoulders would prevent her from rolling too far over its curve.

While he amused himself at her rear the final insult was delivered. In pure horror the nuns gathering around to witness the soiling of their Abbess watched as the sargeant aimed his organ into her open mouth.

Sometime later, after the convent had been looted and the cruel instruments dismantled and loaded back aboard the waggon, the Abbess and her nuns were told to leave, taking only what they could carry. The Inquisitor did not object when the Abbess requested the cart and the rotting sheep carcass to sustain them on their journey.

In single file they set off across the plain, heading for the distant hills. The two whipped nuns rode in the cart, the carcass having been jettisoned as soon as the Inquisition was well out of sight. The rest of the nuns traipsed dejectedly behind.

"Where shall we go?" It was the young lover of the Abbess who ventured to break the depressed silence after some hours of travelling.

The Abbess shielded her eyes from the glare of the setting sun. She could make out a castle on the horizon, a ruin, long abandoned in the plague and where few ventured. "That shall be our new home."

The young nun followed her gaze. "Will we be safe there?"

"We shall be safe and free to continue our order. And as we grow old fresh nuns will take our place, gathered from those unwary enough to stray into our path. We shall not pass away, but will practice our pleasures of the flesh, each generation to the next, getting stronger as the years unfold."

CHAPTER ONE

Late Autumn 1871

"Will you gag me tonight, or would you like to hear me beg for mercy?" There was anxiety in Olivia Holland's voice, there was something pleading.

"I don't know," replied Rupert, feeling guilty that it would be neither of those alternatives.

"You could tie me up if you wish." She could have suggested any number of things that they used to do. The variety of whips and canes, the methods he used to bind her hand and foot before flogging her. She could have done - but she wouldn't; it would be a waste of time and she didn't want to admit that.

"I'll have to see what time I come back from the club. You know how long these meetings take."

But Olivia didn't know, she was never invited anywhere these days, he didn't take her anywhere at all. It might be something to do with the cheap perfume she smelt on his shirts or the exhausted yet contented look in his eyes as he fell asleep without even so much as a 'goodnight'. It was three years since they had married. Only three short years and already he was bedding other women; whores from the Haymarket or the painted trollopes that roamed Picadilly and Oxford Circus.

"I'll dress up for you, if you like." It was a last desperate attempt to entice him back early, away from the wanton legs of the whores and between her own. He used to like having her dressed up, sometimes as a young girl, her hair in bunches, skirts that barely covered her knees, nipples painted pink.

"You could?"

It had failed. There was no interest there either. She knew she was losing her self-control, but that would not do. It would be an admission of defeat. She searched her hand and threw the highest card onto the table; the only one left to play. "You could flog me before you leave," she implored, though she knew that if he did it would only be an exercise to stop her constant moaning - his heart would not be in it. The saving grace was that the sight of her whipped haunches might, just might, excite him enough to penetrate her. Then he might not go to the club.

"Very well. Take off your drawers." There was a flicker of a smile in his exasperated reply. "Fetch the bamboo cane, and be quick." He was thinking of the pretty little whore in the Black Bull, the one with the big mouth. He would have to be quick if he was to get there before she took to the streets. Already she would be putting on her face paint and pulling on her stockings, the ones that reached halfway up her thighs. What was it, he wondered, about a woman's leg that looked so inviting in stockings that revealed an expanse of creamy thigh. The same, he supposed, about a tight fitting corset that made them wasp-waisted and swelled the heave of their breasts. Even the plainest of their sex could look devastating dressed like that. But Laura wasn't plain, that was the trouble, she was as beautiful as his wife Olivia who at that moment was handing him the cane.

While he held it, turning it over and over, running his fingers along its gnarled length, Olivia slipped out of her drawers. She tossed them aside with deliberately gay abandon and bent over the back of a chair. Her arms were straight in front of her, resting on the seat, her bowed head tumbling a mass of splendid raven hair that hid her face completely. He placed the tip of the cane under her falling curls and swept them back over her shoulder. Now he could see her full breasts swing in profile as he caned her bottom. The nipples were erect with anticipation; they poked clearly through the material of her dressing-gown. A fine bead of sweat trickled down her deep cleavage. He was half-tempted to bend and lick it's saltiness, but instead averted his mind to the cane.

Olivia liked it hard, there was no denying that. So he would give it her just as she wanted, without mercy, and by the time he'd finished with her backside she would be begging for him to stop. There was only so much any woman could take, and then perhaps she would leave him in peace. He lifted her dressing-gown and folded it high over her back.

She grunted when the first blow cracked into her buttocks, a blow aimed right across both cheeks where it would sting the most. A weal began to form, a light shade of pink on her pure white flesh.

"You love beating me, don't you Rupert," she said through hair which cascaded down again. Her voice was half-muffled and he didn't hear her properly. The cane whistled through the air and caught her under her left buttock, just above the crease of the thigh. Another pink weal was left in its wake. The first was already turning a deeper shade of red.

"I beg your pardon?" he asked, intending to give her another in a place that would really make her howl.

"I said, you like beating me."

"Of course I do."

The cane came again at full strength, catching her across

the crown of her bottom, at the base of the spine. The howl he expected to wake the dead was no more than a savage hiss through clenched teeth, then, a few seconds later a peculiar snorting sound as she fought off the pain rising in her bottom. The clock in the hallway struck nine. He counted the gongs with mounting annoyance that bordered on panic; Laura would be putting the finishing touches to her lips and lacing up her corset. Outside the front door the coachman would be wondering what was keeping his master. He would have to get this over and done with as soon as possible.

The cane swung into the tops of her thighs and she jerked forward. The chair creaked. Again he hit her, this time on the fleshiest part of her bottom, sinking the cane into her cheeks and leaving a deep red weal. He thought he heard a sob as he whistled the cane across her back. That made her jump, and now she did howl.

"You said I liked beating you," he muttered by way of an excuse, as he saw the weals turning a hideous purple.

Olivia kept silent. This was not quite what she had hoped. Why was he not concentrating on her bottom, the place that made her orgasm and him go as hard as a rock? Instead he was lashing her back, working his way down the protruding spine, seemingly attempting to cause her as much agony as possible.

"My bottom," she pleaded. "Hit my bottom, or under my legs if you desire. But not my back."

Rupert did not desire. He would go on laddering her back and shoulders, making her scream, not from sexual excitement but from unrelenting pain. At the sound of her sobbing he lashed her without respite, striping her between the shoulder-blades and on her sides.

"I've taken enough!" she wailed, rocking uncertainly on her heels.

But something in Rupert had snapped. He was enjoying the beating he was giving her. He no longer felt guilty. She had asked for it, and he would give the ungrateful bitch exactly what she wanted.

She was crying now. Through her tears and sobs she managed to mutter: "Will you stay with me after you've finished?"

When I have finished with you, he thought, there will be little point in staying.

Her back was crossed with stripes, hardly an inch of her flesh was left unmarked. He decided to fulfill her wish and thrash her bottom raw. It really didn't matter if she did recover and fell begging at his knees, begging for his organ inside her. Laura was waiting, that was all that mattered. He heard the clock strike the quarter-hour. Laura would be heading towards the Black Bull. The cane went slashing into Olivia's bottom, six strokes delivered one after the other with such rapidity she hardly felt the pause between them. He whipped under her buttocks, lifting her up on tiptoe, making her long legs tense, the calves and thighs straining as she lifted higher, trying to escape the blows. But in vain. He caught her on the side of her flank and she tumbled forward, losing her balance and hanging over the back of the chair, feet free of the carpet, the weight of her body taken on her stomach. Her hands frantically gripped the edge of the upholstery. "Please Rupert, stop! This isn't love! Why don't you have me?!"

He stopped and wiped the sweat from his brow. On the table near the chair was a decanter of brandy. He reached over her shaking shoulders and unstopped it. Beating Olivia was thirsty work. He was late now and would have to drive straight to the brothel. With luck he might meet Laura on the way. Having her in the carriage was not such a bad idea. He paused and looked at Olivia's breasts. Because of the angle at which she had fallen they were swinging away from her chest, her arms were trailing backwards thrusting her body in a forward motion. Only the chair back prevented her from falling over in a somersault. She was still incredibly beautiful, but they'd been married for three years now, and he naturally required some variety. She was on heat now, he was sure of that, and it wouldn't take a great deal of effort to penetrate her. But if he did that she would want more, and more, and more. Then he would be trapped, held in the vice of her long legs around his back, the heels locked. No, he was not falling for that.

The cane went up under the swell of her breasts and Olivia went with it. Carried by her own momentum she tumbled head over heels and landed in a crumpled, sobbing heap. Ironically, she had landed on her back and stayed there with her legs open, slightly bent at the knees as if he had planned it that way.

"Will you take me now?" she wept.

There was a part of him that almost succumbed to her pleading; that wanted him to kneel between her legs and roger her rotten. Where had he heard that before? Laura, who else. 'Go on, roger me rotten', she often said in her course cockney accent.

"I've done what you wanted," he said, straightening his shirt-cuffs and putting on his coat. "I've beaten you, now let that be suffice."

Her head rolled to one side and she saw his highly polished boots treading towards the door. It opened and closed. The footsteps died away in the passage, the front door opened and closed, and the footsteps came back again on the pavement outside the window. The carriage door slammed and the horses trotted away.

Olivia stayed where she was, on her back with her legs still open. Rupert had gone, leaving her in a sexual coma.

He might at least have had the decency to put her out of her misery. Now there was nothing to do but finish the job herself. In the emptiness and gloomy silence of the drawing-room she felt terribly alone and forgotten. At times like this she was sorely tempted to go streetwalking; to put on paint and stand in doorways whispering to passers-by. On the other hand there was always Granby, the footman. But that would be tempting fate. He was sure to talk. It would be all over London by the next morning; how his Mistress had summoned him and demanded sex. And what about all those marks on her bottom? Rupert would throw her out without a penny. She had no wish to go begging for a loaf like a vagrant. She was too proud to return to her bad old ways.

Her fingers strayed to her sex where it was hot and wet, thc labia sensitive and swollen. She slipped her index finger inside, then took it out again and slipped back all four fingers crossed at the tips. Her thumb searched out her clitoris. She had become something of an expert in the art of pleasuring herself. It could be done almost without thinking; a mechanical exercise that had her gasping and panting, arching her back and digging her heels into the carpet.

To heighten her arousal she sometimes inflicted pain upon herself. It was easily done by placing a stiff hairbrush under her bottom, the bristles were sturdy enough to prick the skin and cause just the right amount of pain. And there were dreams; not those that made her wake-up wet, but those which woke her in the middle of the night desperate to be loved. In the absence of Rupert she could only resort to sex in absentia, the use of anything that came to hand, the handle of the hairbrush or the end of a poker. But in the end it all returned to one thing - or rather the lack of it.

She lay panting on the carpet listening to the clock ticking away the precious minutes of her life; a life that seemed increasingly unfulfilled. It was anger that made her straighten her clothing and summon her maid; anger and frustration. Rupert had told her once how in ancient Egypt high-born ladies would assuage their frustrations on their slaves by whipping them or sticking golden needles into their nipples. Sticking needles into Dorothy might be taking matters to extremes, but she could give her a sound thrashing. All she needed was an excuse.

The maid came scurrying into the room, her face flushed and uniform awry. Olivia didn't need to be told what she had just been doing, it was written all over her face; that tell-tale sparkle in her eye, the blushing cheeks and insolent look.

"When I ring for you I expect you to be here at once," she said as firmly as she could. Being strict did not come naturally to Olivia. "So tell me, what was so important that kept you from answering my summons immediately?"

Dorothy blushed redder. "I was in the parlour, Miss. Polishing the grate."

"Are you telling me the truth?"

"Yes, Miss, cross my heart and hope to die."

"If you are lying your wish may well be granted." She grabbed the maid's wrist. "We shall go down to the parlour and have a look at this grate of yours."

"Please, Miss, you're hurting me."

Olivia paid not the slightest heed, but went on along the passage to the parlour dragging the maid behind her. "The grate has been cleaned," she said, "but not recently, or else why would the tiles be covered in ash. If you are going to lie never take anything in vain."

"Pardon, Miss?"

Olivia couldn't be bothered to explain that a skillful liar always covers the tracks. That was one thing about Rupert;

he was good at that, but then, in his position he didn't really need to cover anything. If he told her he had been with a dozen whores there would be little or nothing she could do about it. The thought made her even more angry than ever.

"I want the truth, d'you hear? The truth and nothing but the truth." And she picked up a bunch of birch twigs used for sweeping the scullery floor. They were fresh and springy.

Dorothy looked very frightened indeed. "I - I was with the butler, Miss," she sobbed.

"Really?" Olivia's surprise was genuine. Miller of all people. He who was a devout Methodist and who had worked in a home for fallen women. "Fetch him."

"I was led astray, ma'am," Miller confessed. "By this chit of a girl who came to my room."

Olivia somehow doubted that, but nevertheless it was worth pursuing if only as a distraction from her present misery.

"Show me how you led Miller astray," she said to the maid.

Dorothy pouted, but hitched her skirts up to mid-thigh. She wasn't very old, seventeen or eighteen perhaps, but then it was sometimes difficult to tell. She had good legs, Olivia could not deny that.

"And what else?"

"Miss -"

"And what else?"

Dorothy unbuttoned the apron of her uniform. She had breasts, but small and pert, as were her bottom-cheeks.

"Did you take off your clothes?"

Dorothy looked at the ashes on the tiles. "I did, Miss."

"In front of Miller?"

"Yes, Miss, I did."

"All of them?"

"Every stitch, Miss. He asked me to."

The butler eyed her maliciously. "I did no such thing, ma'am. I -"

"Get out, Miller."

He was gone in a trice, closing the parlour door behind him as he left.

"I will accept that Miller is probably as big a liar as you," Olivia said duly. "But good butlers are hard to come by. Maids, however, are ten-a-penny. Take off all your clothes and bend over that table."

To the maid's astonishment, Olivia threw off her dressing-gown and picked up the birch twigs. Dressed only in her drawers she stood and watched while Dorothy reluctantly peeled off her uniform.

"And now you can remove my drawers."

"I'm sorry, Miss?"

"I think you heard me quite clearly."

Dorothy pouted that cute pout again, but she knelt before her mistress, slipped her fingers under the drawer-strings, and wriggled the garment down over her hips. They dropped around Olivia's ankles, and her hands 'accidentally' rested on the maid's head, preventing her from rising. She could feel soft breath fluttering through her pubis. Not wanting to alarm her too much she helped her stand and then kicked the drawers away.

"Over the table," Olivia instructed. She was finding it increasingly difficult to maintain a stern air. "Right over, so your bottom is well in the air."

The parlour table was as tall as Dorothy's waist, and so she had to stand on tiptoe to bend forward and lower her breasts to the highly scrubbed wood. She reached forward and gripped the worn edge opposite.

"One dozen, Dorothy. That's your due."

The maid's boyish buttocks tensed with alarm, and tensed an awful lot more as the twigs sailed into them. Olivia used her full strength. Not for nothing had she been flogged many years before in the House of Correction. She knew exactly where to land the twigs to deliver the greatest pain. Dorothy yelped as they struck her almost in the groin. Olivia hopped deftly backwards, avoiding being kicked by the flying legs. She delivered another on the flanks, just below the hips. The slim legs flew again and crashed back against the table leg.

"Keep still, or you'll hurt yourself," Olivia advised kindly, her pretence of anger now forgotten. "Your legs are a little thin, but very pretty," she complimented.

Dorothy strained to look over her shoulder. "Thank you, Miss. I've always had - !"

Her sentence erupted into a howl as Olivia lashed the backs of her thighs. The twigs shattered under the blow and scattered about the floor.

"Remind Miller to order a new birch," Olivia panted. The implement had lost its capacity to sting, so she resorted to using the flat of her hand. She spanked the maid as if she were spanking a naughty schoolgirl. Hard uncompromising slaps that went all around the cheeks and upper thighs. The pale skin turned a mottled pink, red and white. A slapping from Olivia was no light thing, and neither did she tire easily. The spanking seemed to go on forever until Dorothy was reduced to a sobbing, blubbering wreck.

"Off the table, Dorothy," she eventually said, quite out of breath.

Dorothy levered herself up and planted her feet unsteadily on the cold tiles. Her mistress regarded her with an expression the like of which she'd never seen before; her cheeks were glowing, her eyes were a little glazed, and her voluptuous lips were moist and slightly parted. Quite what was going through her mind Dorothy really didn't understand. But it was not her place to question her mistress.

"Stand up straight, Dorothy, while I complete your punishment."

Dorothy squinted and bit her lip as Olivia began slapping her legs. At first the blows were sharp and painful, delivered on her thighs and slowly, very slowly, working their way down to her calves. But as the slaps progressed they lessened in their velocity until they were little more than a gesture.

"Your legs really are quite thin," Olivia remarked again, squeezing the flesh of the girl's calves. Her voice had become noticeably husky.

"Yes, Miss ..." Whereas Dorothy was previously expecting and accepting the punishment for her lie, she was now nervously unsure of her mistress's intentions.

"And your thighs ... very shapely, but so slender." Olivia stood and placed her hands on her young maid's hips. As she squeezed she drew her forward until their bodies touched.

"Open your mouth, Dorothy," Olivia whispered. It was not often - if ever - that she was able to play the dominant role, and she was finding it extremely exciting.

Dorothy obediently opened her mouth, and Olivia pulled her close and kissed her full on the lips. She gripped and squeezed the small buttocks. The maid, astonished at this intimate fondling, put her arms around her mistress and instinctively returned the gesture with adorable charm.

"Where is cook?" Olivia asked a little breathlessly as their lips parted.

"It's her night off, Miss," answered the maid sweetly.

"So it is."

"She's gone to visit her friend - the Cavendish's cook - in Whitechapel," Dorothy offered further.

Olivia smiled and kissed her maid's hot forehead. "My bottom," she rasped, "feel my bottom."

Compared to her own slender buttocks Olivia's felt both wide and rounded. Dorothy's hands roamed freely over the soft cheeks, her fingertips tracing the courses of the recent whipping from Rupert with inquisitive uncertainty.

Olivia winced slightly at the touch. "Do you know what those marks are?" she whispered hoarsely.

"I think you've been beaten too, Miss."

"So I have. And now I need someone to apply a soothing balm to my injured parts. Do you understand?"

They looked at one another in silence and then, as if an understanding had been reached, nodded simultaneously. Leading her by the hand, Olivia made her way back through the quiet house and up to her bedroom. If she was going to seduce her maid far better to do it in the privacy of her own quarters where it was a good deal more comfortable than the parlour and away from prying eyes. Miller, she decided, was not one to be trusted.

Olivia lay on her bed, bottom uppermost, and beckoned for Dorothy to kneel beside her. "I take it men are a great source of comfort to you," she said.

"I like being with men, yes Miss," said Dorothy candidly. "I like them to give me pleasure, and I like to give them pleasure."

Olivia warmed to her crude honesty. "And what about giving pleasure to women?"

She wasn't quite as naive as her lack of years would suggest. "But you've got a husband, Miss."

"Indeed I have, but he isn't here and you are." Olivia handed her maid a pot of perfumed cream from her bedside cabinet, and rested her cheek on her folded arms. She held her breath and waited, and moaned softly as hesitant hands eventually rubbed the cooling substance into her heated buttocks. "Hmm ... that feels very nice," she whispered.

It wasn't every day that a maid was able to gain favours by pleasing her mistress in such a way, and Dorothy knew better than to waste such an opportunity. She massaged and kneaded the glorious bottom before her with great diligence. She watched with intense fascination as the firm cheeks quivered under her touch. She had never seen another woman's bottom, and comparing Olivia's with her own she noticed how deep was the cleft and how generous the fleshy cheeks. Her hands worked methodically up the lightly bruised back. Olivia murmured her satisfaction. While she lay there the awful truth of what was happening hit her like a thunderbolt. She was lying face down on the carpet in her own bedroom having her bottom beaten by a skivvy. She was allowing it to take place at her own command, not resisting but accepting it as if it were all part of the maid's duty to give her employer a hearty thrashing. Was this how far she had fallen, feeling every blow that struck her bottom, each lash stinging and burning, each lash sending a dart of delicious pain through her bottom and legs, not to mention her insides.

As Dorothy scooped some more cream from the pot Olivia rolled over, and casually allowed her legs to loll apart. The two females stared at each other. The whole house seemed quieter than Olivia had ever known it before. She reached out and caressed her maid's young breasts. Dorothy nibbled her lip. Her nipples stiffened beneath the teasing fingers. "Put your head between my legs," Olivia whispered. "Kiss me there."

There was a breathless pause which seemed to last forever, and then Dorothy's flushed face lowered, and her hair tickled Olivia's inner thighs. Olivia filled her lungs and pushed her fingers into that soft hair. Timid hands pulled her knees a little wider apart, and hot breath wafted over her labia. She lifted her bottom off the bed a fraction, waiting for the first beautiful touch ...

"What in damnation is going on in here?!"

Olivia shrieked and Dorothy grabbed the bedspread to her nakedness.

Rupert had missed Laura and all night had been cursing himself for wasting precious time on his wife. Seeing her lying with her legs spread and the maid kneeling between them only added insult to injury. The slap that landed on Dorothy's head sent her sprawling onto the floor. The cane that thumped into the pillow would have brained Olivia had that been Rupert's intention.

"Never in all my days - !" he raged.

Olivia thought Rupert was about to explode. She looked up at him with entreating eyes that only served to increase his anger.

Dorothy wrapped herself in the bedspread and scurried towards the door on all fours. The glimpse Rupert had caught of her between his wife's knees had encouraged quite an erection that needed seeing to. "Stay where you are!" he snapped sternly at the maid without tearing his blazing eyes from his harlot wife. "Olivia - Get dressed and get out of my house!"

Dorothy huddled on the floor and watched her sobbing mistress gather some of her things. There wasn't very much to gather, all things considered; not much to show for three less than happy years of marriage.

CHAPTER TWO

Sister Letitia sat in the tiny waiting-room of Evercreech station, listening to the wind and rain battering the windows. She did not always sit there, sometimes she sat in the parlour of the only inn in the town. Sometimes she stayed a night at the local lodging house. But wherever she chose to be her reason was always the same, and today it was the station. She was waiting for a train, or, more precisely, one of the passengers who would be alighting from it. Unbeknown to the passenger, a telegraph had been sent ahead advising Sister Letitia of her arrival. If the train was on time she would not have much longer to wait.

Six miles further up the line a locomotive hauling a solitary coach heaved out of Bridgewater junction. The young woman sitting alone in her compartment wiped her handkerchief across her mouth and pulled a face. She could still taste the bittersweet essence of sperm on her lips. If the price of freedom meant having to suck a man in a train for sixpence, Olivia did not rate her freedom very highly. Inwardly she cursed herself for being so easily taken in. The man who had offered to carry her baggage had seemed genuine enough, smartly dressed and well-mannered, but then, he would have to be if he intended to rob her as soon as her back was turned. When she came out of the buffet the man had gone and so had her bags, along with her savings hidden in the bottom of the valise. Rupert would have the last laugh after all, she was right back where she started - destitute. She told herself that it was only out of sheer desperation that she performed fellation for the price of a bed. She did not want to think about tomorrow, that would doubtless bring enough troubles of its own.

But while she had knelt half-naked between the man's legs, sucking for all she was worth and letting him fondle her breasts, she had formulated a plan of sorts. Her original intention was to reach the town of Ottery and search out her old friend Flora, who had been with her in the House of Correction and had had the sense to leave London and make her own way in the world. She was apparently doing well as the proprietor of a boarding-house, and although Olivia had not heard from her for some months, she was sure to find her still there. The only problem in reaching Ottery was that it was not on the railway and could only be reached by carriage; expensive. She had already resigned herself to showing her favours to some men in order to raise the fare; low lodging houses would provide the means.

She pulled her cloak tighter around her shoulders and stared absently at the passing landscape. Nothing more comforting than mile after mile of flooded plain dotted with willow trees blasted into grotesque shapes by the howling wind. In the distance she saw a line of low hills with one or two isolated cottages around the bottom. She thought she made out a larger building about halfway up, a castle, or country seat perhaps. It looked partially ruined and she assumed that no one could, or would, want to live there. The desolation brought on fresh curses within herself. Had she been more adroit she could have robbed the man she'd sucked. It would have been easy enough while he bent forward to grope her breasts and thumb her nipples. She could have reached inside his jacket and lifted his pocketbook. Flora would have done so without the slightest compunction, but then, that was why she had done so well.

But Olivia wasn't a thief - she'd make her own way in the world as honestly as she could.

Was whoring an honest living? She had never really thought about it, but considered that it was. After all, it was hard work, sweating on your back ten or twelve hours a day, having more men in a fortnight than most respectably married women had in a lifetime.

Looking at the ruin in the distance she did a quick mental calculation. Half a dozen, no, say a dozen men would bring her in a half-sovereign at least, more if she broadened her repertoire. She might possibly raise a whole sovereign; the fare to Ottery with a couple of shillings left over. A dozen then and no more, she decided, and baring her bottom for whatever they chose to use on her, providing it was not too savage. She did not want to give Flora the wrong impression, or anyone else for that matter. Word that a good-looking whore from London was roaming the countryside might work against her. The idea of being whisked off to the nearest magistrate with a possible six month sentence hanging over her head was not to her liking. She would have to be discreet, and once she had enough money she would vow never to resort to that method of earning again.

She cheered up at that, smiled, and rose from her seat. The train juddered to a halt and she stepped out. Immediately she set foot on the platform a gust of wind snatched away her hat and sent it flying over the wet grey rooftops. With her skirts and hair blowing madly she dived into the waiting-room to let the wind abate before venturing out again.

The room was deserted except for a rather shabby looking woman hogging the fire. It was a situation Olivia was used to, and she knew how to deal with it.

"Excuse me," she beamed, "I would like to share some of that heat."

"Of course," the woman replied, shifting her bottom further along the seat.

She was younger than her clothes suggested, no more than twenty or so, with a pretty oval face and golden curls that peeped from under her shawl. She could be useful if she were local. It would save a lot of precious time if she knew the whereabouts of the nearest lodging house; one that might be suitable for what Olivia had in mind. Tact was what was required here.

"A lodging house suitable for a lady traveler," the girl replied thoughtfully to Olivia's inquiry. "You could try the Three Crowns, but I wouldn't recommend it."

"I just want somewhere cheap and cheerful," Olivia suggested. "Not too expensive, but with perhaps a little company. I'll not be staying long."

The girl nodded thoughtfully. If she had any doubts about Olivia's intentions, her face didn't betray them.

"I'm Letitia," she said amiably, "and I think I know the sort of place you're looking for."

The two of them jumped as the waiting-room door suddenly blew open and a shower of leaves blew in and swirled around the room. The door banged against the wall and then slammed shut again as they watched those leaves which had fallen into the fire burst into flames.

Olivia shivered. She gathered her thoughts, introduced herself in return, and asked if the place she was looking for was very far away.

Letitia shrugged. "About a mile or so, but worth it."

"A mile is a long way in this weather," Olivia observed, turning to look at the rain pouring down the grimy window. "I assume it's outside of the town, if it's that far."

Letitia opened a canvass bag and took out a flask. She unscrewed a cup and filled it with hot tea which she handed to Olivia. Grateful for liquid other than cold water to rid the taste of the stranger lingering on her palate, she drank it quickly. Letitia took back the cup and refilled it.

"Go on," she smiled.

Olivia took the second cupful and sipped it. "Where is this place exactly?"

"The White Garter? It's on the old coach road that used to lead to the coast, but not many stay there now, on account of the railway."

Olivia could not hide her disappointment, it was not what she wanted to hear. The idea of tramping for a mile along a deserted road in pouring rain to an empty bed was of no use at all. The girl had obviously misunderstood exactly what it was she was looking for. She wondered if she should come straight out with it. On second thoughts, she better hadn't. The girl might call the stationmaster and have her arrested for a vagrant.

"I was hoping for a little company," she reminded her, taking another sip and watching for a reaction over the rim.

The girl looked blank and not a little dim. She probably wouldn't understand if Olivia spelled it out in words of one syllable. At that moment she experienced a shiver of panic. It was getting towards twilight, and wherever she was going she preferred to get there in the daylight.

"What sort of company?" Letitia suddenly asked.

"Male company." There, she had done it. For better or worse, her intentions were out.

Letitia's face lit up with the sort of expression a young child gives when it has just understood the meaning of something complicated from the incomprehensible world of an adult.

"Oh. Oh I see now," she laughed. "You feel safer with a man around the place to protect you. Can't say as I blame you. Why only yesterday, right in broad daylight, a woman was -"

"Please," interrupted Olivia, "just tell me the nearest place which rents beds by the night and has men in it. Lot's of them."

"It'll have to be the Three Crowns then," she replied darkly, "and if you're certain about that, I'll show you the way."

Olivia got the distinct impression that the girl had hoped to steer her to the White Garter, but it may have been nothing more than a desire to see her come to no harm. In which case she ought to be grateful.

"I've had a long journey," she offered by way of an excuse, "and I really couldn't face such a long walk."

"There's a coach which passes right by it."

"Just now you said the coaches didn't go there any more."

"Not the one to Bridgewater, no. But the one that goes to Sherston does, twice a week. Today and on Mondays."

A glimmer of hope shone in Olivia's mind. The name Sherston seemed vaguely familiar. "Does it go through Ottery?"

When Letitia replied in the affirmative, Olivia could have wept for joy. "Then I ought to take it, because that's where I'm going, eventually."

"After you have stayed in a place with many men," Letitia remarked slyly.

She wasn't quite so stupid after all. "Well, I need the money," Olivia confessed. "You see, my bags were stolen and I've lost everything. I only have sixpence to my name."

"Then you have enough for the fare to the White Garter. The coach stays overnight," she paused as a smile flickered across her lips. "And so does the driver and the other male passengers."

Olivia blushed. Perhaps it was she who was dim-witted. Letitia might well have been suggesting this all along, but then she didn't know her intended destination was Ottery. Anyway, things had worked out better than she'd hoped. She would be on her way to Flora, and with the opportunity of earning the rest of the fare.

"I really can't thank you enough," she said.

"The coach leaves from the station yard at four o'clock," the girl said. "My train isn't due for another hour, so if I were you I'd hurry along."

Olivia did not need telling twice. She went into the yard and saw the coach making ready to leave. The driver collected her fare and ushered her inside. It swayed on its axles and rumbled out through the station gate.

Sister Letitia smiled to herself as the coach disappeared round a bend and forked off to the White Garter. "You will make a good nun, Olivia," she chuckled quietly, "and a credit to our order. Saint Dulcinea will be well pleased."

There were three other passengers in the coach with Olivia, all men, but little inclined to conversation. But then the journey was a short one, and she could hardly expect them to throw themselves at her, after all, this was not London, and she would have to get used to it.

The inn was set well back from the road, and looked extremely gloomy under the darkening skies. Neither were her spirits raised when the landlord showed her to her room. The ceiling was so low her head bumped the rafters, and the floor had a pronounced slant. The walls were lined with cupboards and dark recesses with doors that hung at crazy angles. All in all, it was a room familiar to anyone who might have sailed on a rotting emigrant ship.

After dinner, which was not at all bad, Olivia tried to engage the men in conversation, but their broad Somerset accents were virtually unintelligible, and the driver, whom she thought had given her the eye, had gone to his room.

She wondered what she had to do to attract their attention. Short of taking her drawers off in public, she couldn't come up with an answer.

At nine o'clock she gave up trying and went to bed. As she stripped off her clothes her mind went back to the man on the train. If all else did fail, she could offer her services to the coachman before breakfast; before the coach set off and left her to walk all the way back to the town. She snuggled under the blankets and pulled them tight around her chest. But sleep did not come easy. The ale she had drunk over dinner played havoc with her stomach, and as there did not appear to be a pot under the bed, she went off in search of a closet. She hoped it wasn't at the bottom of the garden or a bucket in the yard.

The building was much larger than she thought and a veritable labyrinth of passages and stairways, added on over the years with little in the way of any plan. Eventually she found the closet at the end of a passage. She had walked there naked, just in case she did happen to meet any of the men on a similar expedition, but the passages were as still as a grave.

On her return journey she got lost, as she knew she probably would. The narrow passages and winding staircases all seemed exactly alike, and it was a good half-hour before she found her room, the one next to an open cupboard full of mops and buckets. She made a mental note to use one of the latter if she needed to go again.

In the semi-darkness she felt her way along the wall and tripped over the bedside cabinet.

"What the devil - ?!"

Olivia got to her feet, startled. So did the man in the bed. A match flared and hastily lit a candle.

"A thief!" the man exclaimed. "Going through my private belongings!"

"Shhh - please, I'm not a thief," she whispered, trying to calm the man so he wouldn't wake the whole inn. "I've been to the toilet and lost my bearings coming back. I thought this was my room."

She stood resplendent in the candlelight.

"A likely story," he continued in the same angry timbre. "You are either a thief, a prostitute, or a murderess. Which are you? Speak, or I'll call the landlord and have you thrown out into the night as a thief!"

"Oh, no sir! Please, I'm not a thief!" She smiled weakly, quickly seeing the opportunity to earn towards her coach fare. "I - I could be a bit of the second though - if you feel so inclined."

The man leered as the opportunity that had presented itself dawned on him, and reached for her nearest arm. In one swift movement he swung her round, seated himself on the edge of the bed and put her over his knee. Her bottom rested squarely in front of him, perfect for spanking. Her breasts squashed nicely against his outer thigh.

Olivia reached down to the floor to help balance herself.

"First I shall give you a thorough thrashing," he informed her. "And when I've had my fill I shall hand you over to the landlord anyway. We'll see how you like being carted off to gaol in the morning!"

"Oh, no ..!" she pleaded. "Not that. Anything but - !"

He quickly stifled her pleas by stuffing a filthy handkerchief into her mouth. Olivia nearly gagged on the vile odour that filled her palate and nostrils. It was the same taste that she'd washed away with Letitia's tea.

There was a pause while he patted her bottom with great appreciation. Then without warning he smacked her with the full strength of his arm. The shock of the blow almost sent the wad flying from her mouth, but he had stuffed it in too well for that to happen. Slowly she felt the burning of his handprint taking shape on her left buttock. He struck again with even greater force. His palm fell spitefully on her right cheek. And he went on spanking all over her bottom, until it blazed a magnificent hue of bright scarlet. Olivia could feel his thin penis raising against her tummy.

He stopped when he considered her bottom sufficiently coloured, and reached for a jug on the bedside cabinet. Olivia heard him drink and put it back. Thinking her punishment was over, she attempted to heave herself off the floor, away from a large and particularly noisome rat that had come out of its hole to see what was making the row.

"Keep still, you filthy Jezebel!"

Olivia nodded.

"I think your legs need a dose of the same. Would you agree?"

Olivia shook her head, and he thumped her in the small of the back. Getting the message, she nodded frantically.

"Good, I'm glad you agree."

He began again by slapping the backs of her thighs, going down as far as he could reach without toppling over. He slapped her to about halfway down her calves and then worked his way back up, opening her legs and slapping their inner sides. With her legs wide spread, Olivia braced herself for the ultimate blow that would bring fresh tears to her eyes. She held her breath, but the blow never arrived.

Instead of slapping her between her legs, the man put both hands on her bottom and squeezed the cheeks together, making the cleft look longer and deeper than it ordinarily was.

"A fine arse," he complimented.

To show her gratitude, Olivia nodded.

"And good legs too."

She nodded again.

His hands released the pressure on her buttocks, and then prised them as far apart as her flesh would allow. Olivia's eyes widened. She might have guessed what was coming from the way he fondled her bottom. His index finger wormed its evil way into her anus, seemingly testing its depth and girth. He took it out again and returned both index and forefinger, screwing them round and round, tickling the sides and pushing as far as he was able.

"Deeper than I'd hoped," he murmured pensively, as though conducting a highly important experiment and reporting his findings to an assistant. "And nice and snug too." He removed the gag. "I think from now I'd like to hear your sweet voice; its not as common as some."

Olivia flexed her aching jaw, and was just relaxing a little under the rhythmic probing, when without warning she was heaved off the bony knee and tumbled headlong over the bed. Her bottom was in the air, and with surprising agility the man was on his feet and behind her. He kicked her legs open. He seized her arms and wrenched them behind her back where he bound them about the wrists with a belt.

"Before I ride a mare," he wheezed, a little out of breath, "I always give the saddle three hard slaps."

Olivia's bottom wobbled deliciously as he slapped her buttocks in preparation for the ride.

"Now then ..." He sank into her slowly, advancing a little at a time, twisting his hips and moving from side to side, gradually opening her bottom with every little shove of his loins. When she had taken half his length he suddenly thrust forward, filling her completely in one foul swoop. As she gasped and jolted forward into the mattress he wrapped his fingers in her hair and pulled back.

"Argh! Let go - please, you're hurting me!"

Without relaxing his cruel grip the man slapped her flanks

with his free hand. Olivia squirmed on the soft mattress. He took a firmer grip on her hair, and using it like a set of reins, he pulled her head sharply upright. Her eyes watered from the needle-sharp pain in her scalp.

"Is it really necessary to treat me like an animal?" she sobbed.

"How else do I treat a vagrant who comes sneaking into my room?" The man's voice was becoming increasingly strained, and he grunted as he repeatedly pummeled his groin against her splendid buttocks. "By your own admission you're a whore."

"But I - Ooohhh ..." Olivia couldn't suppress a little groan of pleasure. "I'm only trying to earn my fare tuh ... to Ottery."

"In that case you'll have to work very ... umph ... hard ..."

The old bed was straining and squeaking beneath the two sweating bodies.

"... The fare is half a crown, and whores in this part of the country charge no more than a ... oh yeah ... a shilling. So you'll have to put in double the effort!"

There wasn't a lot of effort she could put in - squashed into the bed with her hands tied behind her back and head held rigid. "Wha - what would you like me to do?"

By way of reply he tugged her hair again and penetrated even further. Keeping her head up so that her breasts were strained and her nipples swayed enticingly against the crumpled sheets, he rode her with a steady rocking of his hips; a rhythm that was not violent or rough - and was not unpleasant for her. He was giving her time to get used to his presence inside her bottom, a consideration she was quite unfamiliar with; most - indeed all - men she'd 'known' had thought only of themselves. Between each advance and retreat of his organ he gave a gentle tug on her hair, accompanied by a mild slap on her ribs or shoulders.

Then it came to her in a flash.

"You - you're riding me as if I were a mare!" she exclaimed.

"That's the idea," he replied smugly. "And your arse is just built for riding. Let's see how you go at a canter."

His tempo increased and the bed squeaked all the more.

Olivia was utterly shocked. She had had to be many things in her young life, but never had anyone imagined her to be an animal. Her poor face was a confused cocktail of the undeniable pleasure the penis in her bottom was giving her, and the realization of the role she was playing in the man's fantasy. She had once seen a stallion at stud, and recalled how its huge organ had all but split the poor filly beneath him. The filly had tried to escape, her eyes rolling with terror as the beast plunged home.

The man at her rear was riding her harder now, slapping her around the flanks and ribs and driving into her.

"Please! Please let go of my hair!" she wailed.

The canter had broken into a gallop, increasing the discomfort in her spine, for every thrust of his organ was accompanied by a backward jolt of her head and shoulders.

"Snort, you bitch!" he spat, ignoring her pleas.

It wasn't a difficult thing to do with her hair threatening to rip from her skull, her flanks and buttocks blazing red, and his organ pounding at the walls of her bottom.

"And again!"

Half dazed, her body racked from shoulder to thigh, Olivia obeyed. Tears flowed and blurred the squalid room around her. She was about to scream to rouse somebody in the hotel into investigating the disturbance, when the man suddenly stopped moving. The relief she felt when his hand let loose her hair was a gift from heaven, and she gratefully flopped forward into the mattress. Her wrists were released.

She lay there quietly panting from the exertion. She knew the man hadn't come, and yet the rigid penis withdrew and left her. She peeped sheepishly over her shoulder to see what he was up to now.

"I want you to do it for me," he informed her, seeing the question in her eyes.

"I beg your pardon?"

"I want you to open your cheeks for me, like a good girl."

"I won't," she said with more bravery than she actually felt. "I've had more than I can take of your rude behaviour."

"You'll do as you're told. You still haven't earned your half-crown."

"I've earned a whole sovereign from the way you've treated me."

"You think too highly of yourself, madam. Now, will you open your cheeks, or do I have to persuade you further?"

"Just you try it," she said bitterly, knowing full well that any resistance really was futile.

He knew it too, but her childish stubbornness only added welcome spice to his little game. "I'm giving you your last chance. Spread your cheeks or suffer the consequences."

"Spank me all you like," she defied. "I won't take any more of this. I want to go back to my room."

"I thought you came here with a business proposition. I like whores who honour their contracts."

That was true, they did have a verbal contract, and Olivia's conscience would not allow her to renege upon it. She recognised she had a duty to fulfill, so she closed her eyes, held her buttocks, and slowly eased them apart.

"That's a good little whore," goaded the man. He wanted to gloat in his victory over this beauty.

"Now I suppose you're going to tear my hair out," she

mumbled into her shoulder.

"No, whatever gives you that idea?"

"Oh, I thought -"

"You evidently think and say far too much, young lady. You should learn a little respect."

Olivia wondered how on earth she was expected to respect a man such as this.

"I think a bridle is what is required here."

The belt reappeared and was pulled tight against her closed mouth. "Now don't tell me we're going to have the same trouble as we had with your arse," he sneered.

Olivia kept her jaw firmly clenched. Being ridden like a beast was one thing, being bridled like one was quite another. He could go on slapping her head or wherever else he chose, she would not submit to having his belt forced into her mouth. The blows she expected to knock her senseless did not arrive. Instead, he reached for the water jug and sneakily emptied its icy contents over her head. The belt slipped easily between her teeth as she gasped and gulped for air.

Olivia went on gasping and shivering as the water drenched her hair, chest, and breasts, making her nipples stand up like lead-shot. The belt tightened in her mouth and was pulled taut around her head. She was in a daze as the man entered her again and rode towards his climax. Only the sounds he made told her what was happening. In the midst of his onslaught it occurred to Olivia that if anyone was an animal here, it was surely him.

His harsh grunts rose to a crescendo, and with a mighty shudder he inundated her, filling her bottom and wallowing in it, for no other reason than the pure satisfaction of having defeated all her efforts to resist.

"You can go back to your room now," the man said some minutes later as her unbuckled the belt and removed it from her.

Olivia rolled over and sat on a corner of the bed, as far from him as possible. “What about my money?”

He seemed to have forgotten that. “Oh yeah. Pass me my jacket.”

Grimacing at the earthy odour that came from it, she held it at arm’s length. He rummaged in one of the pockets and flipped her a half-crown.

“I think I’m worth a little more than that,” she ventured.

“I think so too.”

Olivia opened her palm for another coin, but he kicked her in the rump and she shot through the door and ended up in a crumpled heap in the passage. The door closed behind her and was keyed.

“Thank you,” she called aloud. “Thank you very much for nothing!”

CHAPTER THREE

The landlord of the White Garter eyed Olivia suspiciously. He seemed to be uttering some kind of challenge.

“So you went to toilet in the middle of the night, and when you got back, your clothes were gone.”

She stood facing him wrapped only in a sheet. Behind her the autumn sun streamed through the window, silhouetting her contours. Her nipples betrayed her agitation by poking at the material.

“It’s the truth,” she defended. “See for yourself.” She indicated an empty cupboard. “I didn’t notice until I came back from my morning ablutions.”

The landlord shot her a dull glance. “And I suppose

you've lost your purse as well."

"Indeed I have." On the cabinet was the half-crown she'd earned. "That's all I have," she said. "My fare to Ottery."

"And what about my fare?"

Olivia's nipples hardened as they always did when she was frightened. In her excitement of getting to Ottery she had completely overlooked her bill at the inn.

"You may as well take it," she said hopelessly.

The landlord snatched the coin off the cabinet and weighed it in his palm. Then he put it between his rotting teeth and bent it in two. "Lead," he cursed.

"I beg your pardon?"

"It's made of lead - worthless." And he threw it across the room.

"I've been robbed," Olivia blurted, without thinking.

"Oh yeah? By whom?"

Now she would have to tell the truth - the whole truth. It was not a comfortable feeling that gnawed at her stomach. But on the other hand, if the man were still at the inn she could at least confront him, and perhaps the landlord would help if it meant him getting his money for the room.

The landlord blocked the door with his bulk. "Are you suggesting I'm running a brothel?"

"I'm owed what is legally mine," she sobbed.

"I knew it from the moment I saw you. A vagrant. A gutter queen. Well, you're not leaving here until you've paid your bill."

"How can I pay with not a penny to my name?" She instantly wished she had never asked.

"You can start by scrubbing the parlour floor."

"Look," Olivia faltered. "Let me speak to the man in the room at the end of the passage."

"You'll do no such thing. And besides, he left on the morning coach."

Olivia's heart sank. "The coach has gone?"

"At six this morning, while you were still asleep on your back, cooling your arse."

"How dare you."

Without warning or reason he slapped her face, and when she shrieked and put her hands up to her flushed cheeks the sheet dropped to the floor. The landlord gripped her wrist and dragged her naked along the passage and down the stairs to the parlour. Thankfully most of the guests had departed and there was no one to witness her shame.

"On your knees," he ordered.

Olivia fell beside a bucket of water and cloth that had been left in readiness for somebody to use … had this whole scenario been previously arranged? No, Olivia dismissed the idea, it was probably awaiting a cleaner who had not yet turned in for work. "You might at least have the common decency to give me something to cover myself," she said looking up at him.

He threw a towel. Olivia caught it and wrapped it around her waist. It was a small hand towel, ragged and holed, that reached only to her knees. "And for my top half?" she asked hopefully.

"You can stay as you are," her leered and licked his black teeth. "I like the view."

"But it's a little chilly."

He eyed her erect nipples. "I can see."

"You're a pig," Olivia sulked, and then flinched as the landlord raised his open palm as a warning to stop whining and to get on with her chores. Sullenly, she dipped the cloth in the bucket of lukewarm water and started to wipe the floor.

"I said scrub it," the landlord rasped.

When she looked up he was towering over her, and from her place on the floor he looked ten feet tall and very menacing. A scrubbing brush splashed into the bucket from a great height, water soaking her face and breasts and dripping from her nipples. Olivia retrieved it from the water and half-heartedly moved it across the flags. The grime barely lifted.

"Is that the best you can do?"

"I am not a skivvy, sir," she protested. "If you must set me to work, why don't you let me wash the pots or something?"

"You've got a nerve I must say. You try to bilk me of my bill, and then you have the gall to ask for the easiest job going." He grinned evilly. "All right, if you're so keen to wash the pots you can do them after you've scrubbed the floor!"

"But that's not fair!"

"Maybe not, but it's that or the police station for you. Make your choice."

As Olivia set about scrubbing the floor with some degree of diligence the landlord sat at the large kitchen table and tucked into his waiting breakfast. The meal was greatly enhanced for having such a gorgeous wench to watch; her pert bottom raised and her large firm breasts swinging in unison with her efforts.

Olivia eyed the food longingly, and her stomach rumbled.

By the time he had eaten his fill and sat picking bacon from his black teeth the floor was clean and Olivia stood stretching her aching back, unwittingly thrusting her breasts towards his leering face.

"Not bad," he said, surveying the wet floor. "Now the dishes, and then we're almost quits."

"Almost?"

He grinned and nodded to the sink which was overstacked with greasy pots and pans. "Just get on with it - whore," he goaded.

As Olivia immersed her hands into the greasy water in the sink the landlord swung his large booted feet onto the table and sat back with his hands behind his head to enjoy the show. His eyes roamed freely from her long silky hair, over her shoulders and neat back to her trim waist. He farted and adjusted the growing lump inside his heavy corduroy breeches. He checked the wall-clock - the missus would be gossiping with the butcher's wife for quite some time yet. His eyes continued their slow journey, lingering on the torn towel which hinted at the delights of the round rump and shapely thighs beneath, down her slim calves and ankles to her bare feet. As she worked he slipped a hand into his pocket and rubbed his erection. His movements were bold; there was nothing shy about the man. Olivia was concentrating on her work and wasn't watching him masturbate, but he'd have quite enjoyed it if she was. Before long he was almost spurting in his pants, and the temptation of having such a beauty all to himself was too much for such a simple man to resist. He rose and moved to the bin beside the draining-board, his tented breeches leading the way. Holding his plate and the remaining scraps thereon over the bin he spied - as he knew he would - the look of hunger in Olivia's eyes.

"What's the matter with you?" He knew full well.

"I - I'm very hungry, sir," Olivia decided it was time to be polite to the horrible man. "And I have a long journey ahead of me once I've finished here, sir."

"You are?" he scratched his chin.

"Yes sir, I am."

"Well how on earth do you intend to pay for such fine fayre? I have no other chores for you, and you've barely paid for your board and lodging thus far."

"But, they're only scraps." Olivia couldn't believe he was being so unkind - or perhaps she could.

"What nonsense," he put the plate on the drainer and moved behind her, the toweling and the corduroy the only line of defence between her bottom and the tip of his erection. "Many a pig farmer 'round these parts'll give good money for those 'scraps'." His foul breath lifted the soft hair at her temple as he wheezed, "How much are you prepared to give?"

Olivia wasn't prepared to give anything to the odious man. "Please sir, forget the food. I'll just finish these pots and be on my way."

"Fiddlesticks! A young wench like you needs to keep her strength up. There are some despicable scum out there who'll take advantage of such a lovely specimen if you don't have your wits about you."

Despicable scum like you, thought Olivia.

"Besides, you have no clothes. What'll you wear on your journey?"

Damn the man! He was right of course.

"I could get you one of the wife's old frocks …"

Olivia knew exactly what was coming next. The man was very predictable.

"But that too would cost …" Olivia felt his hands wriggle between them to squeeze and mould her buttocks in tight circles, "… naturally."

Olivia sighed with resignation, gripped the edge of the sink, and braced herself in readiness for whatever filthy designs the man had.

"That's better," he wheezed and slobbered in her ear. "You know you want to really. Now, let's have a little bit of fun together."

He lifted her hair and wetly kissed the nape of her neck. Despite her abhorrence Olivia's treacherous spine tingled. He leaned into her back and trapped her against the sink. The buttons and rough material of his shirt agitated her skin. One callused hand slid between her arm and her flank and fumbled for her unprotected breasts, and Olivia felt the other opening his breeches. She felt his stalk spring out against her bottom, and then the hand gathered up the towel until it was able to snuggle between the tops of her slightly parted thighs.

"Lean forward a little," the landlord croaked.

Olivia did as he demanded, until the last remaining soapsuds in the sink burst and tickled her hanging nipples. He gave himself some room, and then Olivia felt his smooth round helmet nudge into her labia. He blabbered something incoherent into her ear and filled her with a couple of crude stabs. Olivia was most uncomfortable. Her hips banged against the hard edge of the sink and she struggle to get her legs wide enough apart so as to ease his access. He started to pump in and out, levering her hips back and forth, and she could tell the useless oaf wasn't going to last very long. His breathing bubbled in his chest and his legs trembled against her own. Her hips continued to bump uncomfortably against the sink as he lay across her back and forced her breasts further down into the greasy water. He grunted and rutted like one of the pigs that might enjoy his scraps. Despite Olivia's loathing of the man she felt her own wicked excitement rising.

"Don't come yet!" she implored, needing a few moments more to reach her own peak of pleasure.

"Too late!" he bellowed. "Oh God - too late!" and he withdrew and Olivia felt his hot seed splatter onto her back and haunches. She groaned and clutched the sink edge all the harder, but as her unfulfilled passions subsided she felt immense gratitude to the oaf for being so sensible with his emission. She reached blindly behind her and stroked his softening member to convey her appreciation to him. It seeped some more seed into her palm and she smoothed it back and forth. Perhaps she could coax it back to full glory, and then if she blanked its owner from her mind and fantasized about a dream lover she may be able to quench the yearning that had initially been stirred during her encounter with the equestrian fanatic.

"Well, well, well. What do we have here then?"

Olivia's heart sank further at the sound of a gruff female voice. Was it her misfortune to be interrupted at the most inopportune moment for the second time within a week? The landlord hastily pulled away and left her sticky hand clutching thin air.

"Oh - hello dearest," he slavered sickeningly. "I - um - I was just checking the wench's work."

"Wasn't all you were checking!" snapped the lady of the house, spying his pathetic prick poking from his breeches and Olivia's creamed bottom. "Get out of here, before I take my hand to you!"

"Yes dearest," he backed away from the barrel of a woman. "I was just going anyway."

Olivia stood and watched him scurry from the parlour with contempt. Greasy water dripped from her nipples. The wife approached and glared at her.

"You little hussy!" she spat. "Can't you find a man of your own without having to seduce married men?!"

Olivia couldn't believe her ears. "But - he - I -" Her indignant stammering was abruptly cut short by a sweeping right hook which boxed the side of her head. "Ouch!!" she wailed.

"Get out of here before I really lose my temper!" screamed the stocky wife.

"But -"

"Out!"

"But what about some clothing?"

"Sacks!" bellowed the wife. "In the outhouse! And think

yourself lucky I'm so considerate!"

"This isn't fair," moaned Olivia. "I don't deserve this."

"What you deserve, young hussy, is a spell in the workhouse. Now be off with you before I change my mind and have you arrested for whoring!"

Olivia fled as fast as her stumbling legs could run. She stopped by a water-butt and washed away the landlord's drying residue. The sacks were piled up in one corner of the outhouse and she selected the largest she could find. Above them was a shelf with tools on it. She rummaged amongst them and found an old rusting bread knife. It was just sharp enough to slit the sack up its seams. She tied it around her middle with a piece of twine, and then taking another, she slit it and wrapped it under her arms. It was extremely uncomfortable, but at least she was covered. She put the knife back on the shelf, changed her mind, and hid it under her waist; it might prove useful. If she had to go abroad looking like a vagrant, she may as well act like one.

CHAPTER FOUR

Barefoot and once again alone, Olivia set off. At least the weather was a little kinder than the previous day. When one is brought so low and can go no lower, care goes out the window. As Olivia walked along the wet verges on the side of the road, where the grass was kinder on her feet, she was past caring what people thought of her. The only thought was to keep going and reach Ottery as soon as possible. The drivers of the occasional waggon or cart that happened to rumble by never so much as gave her a glance;

perhaps beggars and female vagrants clothed in old sacking were a common sight in this part of the country. She did eventually manage to hitch a lift on a passing van. The driver didn't utter a word, but kept his eyes on the nag, lazily flicking his whip now and then.

It was after midday when she was dumped at a crossroads. There was only one dwelling in sight, a lonely cottage standing in the middle of a field. On a line in the garden the morning's wash fluttered in the breeze. The instincts of self-preservation rose to the fore. Vagrants lived on their wits, and so must she. It wasn't difficult reaching the cottage unseen. All she had to do was whip the clothes off the line and run. She was almost giggling with relief as the pegs flew hither and thither. The calico dress spotted with daisies was a little small, but the drawers would fit. She carried them to a shed and quickly stripped off. Deciding she wouldn't need the knife any longer she left it on the workbench.

Although the back door to the cottage was open, she sensed it was deserted. Perhaps the occupants were at work in the fields. Her raging hunger suddenly demanded attention. She would not take anything of value, just a loaf from the kitchen and a handful of apples.

Feeling much more civilized in her stolen clothes and cheered by her armful of bread and fruit, she stepped from the kitchen into the sunshine.

"Afternoon."

Olivia froze in the doorway. "Oh ... good afternoon," she replied stupidly.

As the man slowly advanced Olivia slowly retreated until her bottom bumped softly against the kitchen table. The apples fell from her cradled arms and bounced across the floor. She blushed and placed the loaf on the scrubbed worktop she leant against. "Look ... I can explain ..."

What was there to explain? That she had just stolen the morning's wash, had dressed herself in someone else's clothes, and had robbed the kitchen?

In the awful silence that followed the cottager went to the sink and washed the mud from his hands.

What was he? A farmhand, perhaps?

The powerful chest that bared itself from under his open shirt was swarthy and tanned. The sweat that rose from his body had an earthy smell about it. He didn't seem particularly disturbed at finding an attractive young woman in his kitchen, neither was his voice harsh when he told her to take off the clothes and put them back where she'd found them.

"Of course, sir." Olivia felt extremely humble. "Would you mind if I put my sacking back on? I have nothing else to wear."

But when they got to the shed the sacking wasn't where she had left it. Only the string she'd used to keep it about her was still there.

"Pick it up," the man told her with the same melodious drawl.

Naked, now that the clothes were folded neatly where her knife had been, Olivia bent low and picked up the string. She obediently padded in front of him down the garden path, like a docile beast driven to market, the string in hand.

"Put your arms around that post," he told her.

Olivia could have probably outrun him if she chose to flee. He might be fit and strong, but she was a little taller and lithe as a gazelle. She could run like the wind when she had to. But where would she go? Back to the inn, or to the ruined castle she saw on the side of the hill? It was closer now and she could make out windows in one of the towers and what she assumed was the gatehouse. She'd look a fine sight, running stark naked across the countryside towards an old ruin.

"I think you're going to beat me," she volunteered, pressing her body against the post which held the washing line and putting her arms around it.

"I could call the constable."

Why was it that whenever she found herself in difficulties people always threatened her with magistrates, constables and prisons? So far, no one in this inhospitable landscape had offered any alternative. The world, she decided, was a harsh place, peopled with uncaring souls whose only ambition was to chastise her at the first available opportunity.

"There. That'll do."

He smiled the sort of smile he'd probably give if he'd just sold a beast at enormous profit, one that was likely to drop dead the very next day. He'd made a good job of tying her hands; if she as much as moved an inch the string would cut into her flesh. The sun was well up and for an autumn day was quite strong, warming her back and bottom. Her feet rested on soft damp earth, and the man seemed to be going out of his way to make her comfortable when he lifted them by the ankles, one at a time, and removed his shirt and put it beneath them.

"You're a lady," he observed rather astutely. "An' I always treats a lady right."

"Oh, thank you," she replied, taken aback by the admission.

He left her tied to the post and went back into the cottage. She could hear a cupboard door opening and the sounds of rummaging within. He was whistling happily to himself as he went about whatever he was doing. Maybe she wasn't going to be beaten after all. Perhaps he was going to do nothing more harmful than leave her there for a few hours to ponder her misdoing. It certainly made a change. He was gone a long time - long enough for a cart to appear on the horizon, travel along the road and go past her.

"Lovely afternoon," the driver called cheerily and waved his whip.

"Lovely," Olivia called back absently.

After he had passed it occurred to her that perhaps the man in the cottage often served his wife in the same way, and it was therefore no surprise to find a naked woman bound to a post in the garden.

The man came out of his cottage and down the garden path. "Sorry to keep you," he apologized most civilly. "Couldn't find what I were lookin' for." But without further ado what he had found slashed into her buttocks with the fury of a maniac.

"What are you using on me?!" she shrieked in alarm.

The belt was a broad strip of leather, about three feet long and four inches wide. The brass buckle at the end could have fitted over both her palms. He held it up for her to look at. Olivia gulped. "It's a harness," he told her, evidently proud of its highly polished sheen.

"A thing like that will kill me," she faltered.

He went behind her, gathering the harness for a fresh strike. There was no malice in his eyes or curling of his lip. He was going about it matter-of-factly, as if he did it every day of his life.

"A woman," he told her, "is like a walnut tree. The more you whip 'em, the better they be."

Olivia had heard of that; walnut trees being whipped at their trunks to make the sap rise. She couldn't quite see the logic of that comparison. What on earth did he hope to rise in her?

"I'll give you twelve," he said. "Then you be 'bout ready."

Olivia's jaw dropped in dismay. "Ready for what?"

"You know."

She didn't know - not a clue. And neither did she much care at that moment. It was impossible to contemplate anything except the belt whistling into her bottom like lightning. In the stillness of the warm afternoon the sound it made seemed particularly emphatic; a deep hissing which terminated abruptly with a dull thump, followed by a piercing shriek. Olivia twisted and turned and writhed to escape the scorching lashes. All she could manage was to slowly work her way around the post, one foot at a time, but to no avail; he merely side-stepped her, keeping pace with her movements. Gradually it dawned on her that there was a purpose to his whipping. The more her hips gyrated the greater the lashes. She became more and more aware of the splendid spectacle her naked and squirming body presented. Every time he sent the belt slashing into her bottom, her whole body broke into a dance of agony. She hugged the post in pain, snaking her hips and breasts against it. The wood, although fairly smooth, had excited her nipples as they rubbed to and fro. To anyone who happened to pass it looked as if she were mad or demented. Neither did her moans and pants help matters. Her face was flushed from the exertion of trying to escape the lashes that now landed on her thighs. He hit from left to right, alternating each stroke to coincide with the swing of her hips. It was no steady sway but an abrupt, burning jolt, that drew attention to the splendid contours of her bottom and back. A Turkish odalisque would have been hard pressed to match the twisting of her spine and the undulation of her shoulders.

He was a virile male of flesh and blood, and it was no surprise that the sight of her contortions had given him an enormous erection. He came up behind Olivia and she felt his knarled stem rubbing and throbbing into her bottom cleft.

"There," he panted, slightly breathless from his own exertions. "I told you a woman was better for a good whippin'."

Olivia did not feel better. She was close to exhaustion. Near to collapse she sagged against the post, her head to one side, scarlet and flushed.

"I don't know what you mean," she sobbed. "How can I feel better after being whipped with that thing, and my body aching all over?"

"I didn't mean you."

A baffled expression crossed her face. "Well, what can you mean?"

To demonstrate his meaning he slapped her left thigh where the welts were thickest; where the pain was most acute. Her hip jerked away from his hand and he instantly slapped the other thigh.

"There, see now?"

Olivia still hadn't caught on.

He slapped her bottom with the flat of his hand, making her hug the post all the more. Her groin twisted against it and she groaned. That encouraged another harder slap. The groans grew louder and longer. The wood now grazed her breasts and nipples, but she was oblivious to the growing soreness there.

"I could slap yer arse all day long," he gasped close to.

Olivia strained to look over her shoulder, and through moistened eyes saw him stand back to admire his handiwork with undiluted lust etched on his weathered face. At that moment, as if someone had just whispered in her ear, the answer came; she suddenly understood the meaning of his words. She had been whipped not so much as a punishment, but more for the spectacle she had presented as she writhed and twisted at the post. It must have been highly erotic;

watching her every contortion of hips, thighs and back. No wonder his erection reared up at her from his open breeches. A bizarre measure of pride rose within that her body was so beautiful, and could so readily excite such a massive erection. She wondered what he now planned to do with it.

"What are your intentions, sir?" she asked with meek respect.

"Why," he grunted, "what would you have me do?"

"I would rather you do nothing more. I would rather be on my way if you don't mind, so please untie me."

The man looked at the sky and thoughtfully stroked his chin. The sun was already descending towards the horizon, and the shadow of the post was slowly lengthening.

"It'll be dark afore you reach anywhere," he advised. "You can't travel at night. Too dangerous with all these beggars 'bout."

"I am grateful for your concern, but if you hadn't delayed me in the first place I wouldn't have to worry about that."

"If you hadn't bin stealin', I wouldn't 'ave delayed you."

Olivia couldn't really argue with that observation.

"Well, what am I to do?" she asked.

"You can stay 'ere the night, where I can keep an eye on you."

"What about your wife? What'll she have to say about that?"

He didn't answer.

Olivia felt a wave of relief wash over her; perhaps the wife had gone away somewhere for a few days, and with luck she would now get a hot bath and a meal. There was no reason why she should not. She had been punished and had satisfied his curious penchant for watching her writhings. The erection had not subsided, and she knew she may have to show her gratitude for a hot meal, a bath, and a good night's rest. But it would be worth it.

"Well, thank you kindly, sir. I don't mind sleeping on the floor." She thought it best not to appear too forward.

"Eh?"

"If you haven't got a spare bed, I don't mind the floor," she repeated, tugging at the string.

He scratched his head a little stupidly and gave her a queer look. "How can you sleep on floor tied like that?"

"Well, of course I have to be untied first," she said, struggling to keep her patience.

He still scratched his head, trying to fathom her meaning. His boot kicked at the damp earth. "You'll catch cold down there," he remarked. "But it's up to you."

Olivia looked at the garden, then at him, and finally at the post. "You mean, I'm supposed to stay here all night, tied up like this?"

"Safer than walkin' the countryside in dark."

"But - but what if someone should come?"

"They won't see yer from road - not in the dark."

His logic infuriated her. "What if I were to sleep in your cottage, wouldn't that be better than leaving me here all night?"

"Don't trust yer," he said flatly.

"But - I'm really very harmless!" Olivia was getting somewhat desperate at the thought of staying outside all night.

Quite unexpectedly he untied her wrists and made her kneel in the dirt. His organ hovered in front of her eyes. "Okay little missy, show me why I should trust yer."

"How should I show you? Want do you want of me?" Olivia knew exactly what he wanted of her, but guessed a little coyness would help dissipate his suspicions toward her.

He remained silent, looking down at her. Her tired limbs

and empty stomach implored her to do as he wanted. Without another word she reached for him, closed her mouth over his organ, and started to suck - careful not to graze him or give the slightest excuse to keep her tied up in the garden all night. He gripped the post with both large hands and leant over her. His thighs agitated her sore breasts. Her tongue furled around the plum and she swallowed the length to the back of her throat. She began to wonder if his body was as senseless as his head seemed to be, for no matter how hard she worked or whatever little tricks she used, he was clearly no nearer reaching his climax after she'd been on her knees for a good ten minutes. Her jaw ached and her knees ached. She was at the point of asking why she obviously wasn't pleasing him, when he suddenly groaned like an ox and filled her surprised mouth with one pulse of his mighty weapon. Olivia squealed at the amount she was having to swallow, but soon his wet organ slipped from her lips and he stood panting with his forehead against the post. He stood like that for some minutes. Olivia wondered if he was all right, or whether such a generous ejaculation had drained him of his strength. Such a display of virility she had never before witnessed - or enjoyed.

"You'll do," he eventually mumbled, and helped her to her feet.

"Do you treat your wife like this?" she ventured to ask as he stooped to pick up his shirt. "Tying her up and whipping her?"

"Never married," he grunted.

"Then whose clothes - ?"

"None of your business!" he snapped, slapping her face.

Olivia reeled from the sudden and harsh blow. That was another thing she was getting just a little sick of - people using her as a punch-bag. "What was that for?!" she wailed, rubbing her burning cheek.

"Don't ask questions! Not if you want to stay here the night!"

CHAPTER FIVE

Olivia awoke just before the dawn. She was alone in the bed, although the sheets next to her were still warm. Her neck, arms and back ached, and her bottom throbbed. She sat up and rubbed her chafed wrists, noticing for the first time the tender abrasions on her breasts. She wondered, with a twinge of disappointment, why the man had made no further attempts to touch her during the night, but at least she had enjoyed his food and the tub of steaming water.

She rose from the snug bed and went to the bedroom door. "Hello?" she called softly. Then in a louder voice, "Hello? Are you there?"

Silence. Perhaps the man had gone to work.

She found an assortment of frocks and underwear in a wardrobe, and hastily dressed without paying too much attention that she was respectably covered.

The only other room along the landing was empty and needed airing. She cautiously went downstairs. The parlour was through a door to her left. There was no furniture of any kind in there - not even a chair. Strange, she thought, but no matter how much she tried to convince herself otherwise, it was obvious that the cottage had been virtually empty and without a woman's touch for a very long time, perhaps years even. Then why all the female clothing? They obviously didn't belong to him ...

She went out to the garden and picked up the belt. Thank

God it was real, or else she really would have thought herself mad. The string which had been used to bind her were gone. There was something very peculiar about this place.

Olivia hoped desperately that the cart approaching in the distance would stop and give her a lift; she didn't want to stay a second longer.

The cart was in fact a small covered waggon, and when it stopped Olivia's heart almost accompanied it. In the back, where the driver motioned her to go, were two women dressed all in black, their heads covered under hoods. Once aboard and beside them Olivia felt very foolish in her ill-fitting outfit.

"Good morning, child."

"Thank you for stopping," she replied, feeling obliged to offer an explanation for her disorderly appearance. "I'm afraid I was robbed on the highway, and left only with this old frock."

"Dear me." And the woman leaned with an ease of movement to close the canvass over the back of the waggon.

Light came through a small window in the side illuminating a golden cross hanging from a chain around the woman's neck. Her companion was similarly adorned.

"What are these marks about your breast, child?"

Olivia looked down at the upper slopes of flesh which the frock failed to cover in the half-light. She tried to pull the thin material about her bursting bosom.

"I - I was beaten by my attacker," she said, telling the truth for once.

"Then you must let us take care of you. Take off those clothes and we'll see what we can do."

She had no hesitation in stripping off her rags, although she did wonder exactly what these two women could do to help. It was a little awkward undressing in the rocking waggon, but she cared not for she felt safer now than she had done since first stepping off the train. The nuns showed no reaction whatsoever to her nakedness, but opened a casket and retrieved a bottle of ointment.

"Now child, sit between us, and together we shall heal your wounds."

It felt odd to be addressed in such matronly terms. From what she could see of them the one speaking was a handsome woman, and the other was younger and prettier. They both looked rather young to have taken up holy orders, but, Olivia supposed, everyone had to start somewhere. She wondered what had induced them to take it up.

The pretty nun sitting on her right tipped a little of the ointment in her palm and began rubbing it into Olivia's corresponding breast. The handsome one on her left took the bottle and repeated the procedure, rubbing it into the other breast.

"You're both very kind," Olivia mumbled, relaxing against the side of the waggon.

Their hands moved in unison; a gentle rubbing of palms over her nipples and getting wider, going in concentric circles, gradually covering both breasts completely with the soothing ointment.

"We must attend to these little bruises," one of them whispered.

"We must," the other agreed.

"I think it would be best if you laid on the bench opposite," continued the first, "you're in much worse condition than we thought."

Their tone had an air of professionalism, rather like a doctor who although kindly, expects his command to be obeyed. Rather dreamily, Olivia seated herself on the bench, her legs together, hands in her lap.

"Lie down, miss," said the older nun. "We can't treat

you while you sit up." Her tone was such that Olivia quickly obeyed as a child responds to a firm governess.

A finger was applied to her nipples. It slowly moved round and round the teat; a touch like velvet. Olivia held her breath as her nipple rose up hard and tingling.

"Very good," the pretty nun observed. "Your flesh responds well to treatment."

Olivia gazed up into her face. It was the face of an angel, and when she smiled her lips spread wide, revealing neat white teeth. Her lips were particularly well shaped; a perfect and sensual bow. They closed in a pucker, the lower lip pouting slightly, and then before Olivia could grasp what was happening the nun's face lowered and her mouth closed over her nipple and sucked it in.

The gasp of surprise Olivia might have uttered was stifled by a pair of fingers slipping into her own mouth. She gazed at the swaying canvas roof, sucking obediently and being sucked in return. The nuns certainly knew how to take care of their sick patients. The soothing fingers moved very slowly and seductively in and out of her mouth. The lips sucking her nipple drew it in with a delicious kiss. The naughty tongue flicked over the pulsing teat.

Olivia couldn't suppress a soft groan. A wonderful feeling of weightlessness seemed to flow through her aching body. Already the torments of the previous day were beginning to subside.

"Rest, child." The voice of the handsome nun whose fingers she sucked was almost hypnotic. Olivia felt her eyelids growing heavy. "Lie back, safe in the arms of those sent to save you."

"You are saving me," she muttered.

Their voices seemed to be both near and far. Their hands wandered over her chest and belly, yet felt as if they were merely hovering. She had just the amount of strength left to answer their questions. They came one after the other, from each in turn, so it was difficult to fathom who was actually addressing her. It hardly mattered, for their faces and voices had fused into one. The hands that roamed over her body did not feel as flesh and bone, but something she could not quite describe.

"London …" she murmured. "I came from London … on the train."

For a fleeting moment another face flickered through her mind, someone she had met at the little country station, but in a flash it was gone. She could feel her breasts being tenderly squeezed, and her nipples lightly thumbed.

"You're visiting relatives, then?"

"A friend," she muttered. "Flora ..."

The hand that was now stroking her thigh suddenly tensed. Olivia tried to sit up but was held firmly by the shoulders. She was being massaged, the fingers that were in her mouth now manipulated around her neck and throat. The insides of her thighs started to quiver.

"And you were attacked and beaten on the highway?"

"Not the highway exactly … at a cottage." It was impossible to lie to those gentle faces and the hand progressing further into her groin.

"A cottage?"

"I was caught borrowing some clothes. The man there tied me up and punished me."

"Were not your own clothes sufficient?"

"They were stolen at the inn - the White Garter. A horrible man took advantage of me and my clothes were stolen."

"I see," whispered the handsome nun as she soothed Olivia's hair. "And you left there and tried to steal some more clothes from a cottage."

Olivia knew it must be difficult to believe her story. "Yes.

The cottage where you picked me up."

"Yes … of course."

She felt they were finding it difficult to accept her explanation, and she didn't want two such kind people to think of her as a liar. "He beat me with a belt." She hesitated, trying to remember. "No, it was a harness. A thick one with a big buckle on the end."

A hand crept under her thigh and gently lifted, stroking as it eased further away from the other. Her legs were open before she realized. Hands still cupped both her breasts and squeezed firmly.

"And your friend, Flora - where does she live?"

Olivia squealed softly and her belly heaved as a tongue swept across her labia. "Is - is this part of your treatment?"

"Tell me about your friend," the dreamy voice coaxed.

The tongue found her clitoris. Through mists of pleasure she wondered why they were doing this to her. It had been her back and bottom that had been welted, not her groin. "An old friend …" she answered vaguely. "Lives in Ottery … Luckily I memorized the address … otherwise I'd have lost it when I was robbed."

"You still have a long way to go then."

She gasped as her clitoris was sucked between the wonderful lips. "You're making me come," she moaned. Her thighs tensed and she groped blindly for the side of the waggon. Her hands were seized and held tight as she started to rise to her climax. The questions ceased, giving her time to reach and pass her orgasm. At the point where the unselfish lips were about to bring her off, Olivia opened her mouth and it was instantly covered by another. She was kissed passionately for a long, long time, until she had reached her orgasm and lay panting and gasping, her legs hanging limp from the bench.

"Thank you …" she whimpered. "You're both very

kind."

"Turn over," said one of the nuns; Olivia wasn't sure which one.

"What more are you going to do?" she asked feebly.

"See to your wounds; the places where you were belted with the harness - or whatever it was."

"It was a harness. He hit my bottom with it while I was tied to a post."

"A post? You didn't mention a post."

Olivia didn't want these two angelic souls to doubt her, so she said no more and rolled over onto her stomach.

"My, you have been beaten."

Olivia sensed a curious tone to the nun's voice. "Yes - I have."

Without another word they dribbled the ointment over her back and buttocks. Again they worked in unison. Two hands rubbed her back, covering it completely from shoulders to hips, from where the others took over and smoothed her buttocks. Fingertips worked furtively into her cleft, probing quietly into her back entrance.

"You said I still had a long way to go," she reminded them weakly, shuddering as the finger wormed just inside.

"Did we?"

"Ottery. You said Ottery was a long way from here. The girl at the station said it was ... Ooohhh!" The finger sank slowly and Olivia arched her back as much as the restraining hands would allow. She held her breath, knowing precisely what was coming. "Oh, God," she panted, as more fingers smoothed over her labia and then two or three slid inside. Her bottom and vagina were filled with slick digits which twisted and revolved in unison. She assumed making her orgasm was all part of the treatment; a clinical exercise to make her feel more relaxed. But before she was able to reach her peak the delightful tormenting disappeared. Olivia felt empty and ached for release. "Are you finished?" She hoped they weren't. To her secret joy hands wormed between her stomach and the bench and rolled her over.

"We just have your legs to do."

She felt intensely close to the two women as they completed their considerate therapy. She suddenly had a thought, and asked tentatively: "Do you live in that old castle on the hill?"

"We do. It's our convent." The more motherly of the two cradled Olivia's head while her companion kneaded the remainder of the ointment into her legs. Through the dark tunic Olivia could feel a firm breast moulding against her hot cheek. She sensed they were awaiting her next question.

"I don't suppose," she whispered, "that I could stay at the convent until I recover fully and can get word to my friend. I'm sure she would bring me some clothes and help me pay for my board."

The two smiled at each other knowingly. "You are more than welcome to what small comforts we can provide, and you will pay for nothing."

Olivia wanted to hug them both. "You are so kind! You are so unlike all those other horrible people I've met!"

The waggon rolled and clattered over a drawbridge, and she could see through the back of the canvass a crumbling gatehouse and the surrounding walls of a courtyard.

"Here we are," said the motherly nun.

"Can I ask …" ventured Olivia one last time, "… who are you?"

The nun smiled down kindly and stroked her brow. "We are known as Dulcinites, after our patron saint Dulcinea - the bringer of pleasure."

CHAPTER SIX

Olivia bethought herself back in the House of Correction when she saw her cell. It was primitive in the extreme; a rude bed with a horsehair mattress, a slop bucket in the corner, and a stone basin to wash in. The tiny barred window overlooked the courtyard that had once been the inner bailey of the castle. A peculiar contraption stood in the middle of it; something resembling a gibbet, except it was tee shaped with chains hanging from either end.

Still, she thought, it didn't matter what the place looked like, or its conditions - she wouldn't be there for too long. She presumed there was a telegraph somewhere nearby, and then it wouldn't take Flora more than a day or two to send money and clothes. She ate a plate of stew and then settled down for the night under the grey blankets on the rigid cot.

In the morning she was awakened by a nun with a plate of porridge and some clothes; a habit, lighter in colour than those worn by the kind nuns who had invited her into their home.

"It's the colour the novices wear," the young nun informed her, "until they are out of their Novitiate."

"I won't be here that long," Olivia smiled.

The nun did not register the remark and told her to eat quickly and attend mass in the chapel. Olivia threw on the blue-grey habit and scoffed her porridge. While she was there it would only be polite to observe the rules, however onerous they might be.

She followed the nun barefoot into the chancel. The whole building was ablaze with brightly painted frescos, and Olivia could not help but wonder at their beauty. Adam and Eve stared from the wall; the serpent coiling around her voluptuous body with its tongue licking at her open legs. Original, thought Olivia. Above the chancel arch the damned were entering hell, all of them naked and being tortured with demons wielding hot tongs and pincers. The faces of the women were ecstatic. The more gruesome the torture the greater their pleasure, especially those being impaled on outrageously enormous male organs. It was the same everywhere. Even the severed head of John the Baptist looked up with longing into the open legs of Salome as she danced over him. Olivia thought it was all a little bizarre, as a gong boomed out.

The assembled nuns stood as the Abbess walked gracefully up the aisle to the altar, where she stopped, bowed and turned. Olivia imagined her to be some wizened old woman who had been there for the best part of a century. Instead she saw a stunning woman of no more than thirty with sculptured cheek-bones and sparkling eyes. Her slightest movement sent her habit shimmering from the tips of her noticeable nipples. It was beautifully made from black silk and seemed designed to show off her seductive figure. She was so extraordinary that Olivia found it impossible to tear her eyes away. So did, apparently, all the other nuns, who gazed at her with rapturous adoration. When she spoke her voice was smooth and resonant.

"We have a heretic amongst us," she announced with ease, "who refuses to obey the rules. Heretics must be punished."

Olivia froze on the uncomfortable pew. For one awful

moment she thought the Abbess was looking at her. But the beautiful face turned and the sparkling eyes fell on a nun seated on the other side of the aisle. Olivia was sure there was something untoward happening here, but something she had not quite grasped. A shiver ran down her spine.

"Come forward, Sister Lizabet," the Abbess commanded. The nun called Sister Lizabet rose, bowed, and walked to the front.

The seated congregation craned necks and peered around those in front to see all the better. Some knelt on the pews and those at the back stood up. Olivia, seated on the end of her pew nearest the aisle, had an uninterrupted view of the proceedings.

"Take off your habit," the Abbess ordered, and Olivia watched wide-eyed as the nun unknotted the cord around her waist. She let it fall to the stone floor and then, taking her habit by the hem, drew it up and over her head. As she cast it aside Olivia touched a hand to her mouth to suppress the gasp which threatened to draw attention to herself. She was naked! The attractive nun was naked under those robes! Olivia blushed and peeked furtively at the nun sitting by her side. She could clearly see hardened nipples rising against her habit as well! Resting in the deep valley between those pointed and gently heaving breasts was not a crucifix, but a pendant whose design Olivia could not discern. When she lowered her eyes fresh horrors awaited. The nun's robe had fallen open to reveal a pair of bare and shapely legs. The naked thigh pressed against her own, and even through her habit she could feel how warm it was.

An occasional thigh could be seen further along her row as more habits slipped open, and it was the same on the other side of the aisle. For the first time Olivia noticed that all the nuns wore the same design of pendant between their breasts.

"As is our wont," the Abbess spoke and drew Olivia's attention, "disbeliever's may choose how they wish to be chastised." She looked at the naked nun, who stood meekly with bowed head. "Make your choice - the wheel or the whip."

She chose the whip, leaving Olivia to wonder what sort of punishment was delivered on a wheel. Whatever it was, it could not have been worse than the whip now being brought forward. Disgusted at the spectacle, yet irresistibly fascinated, Olivia watched the naked nun lift a cat o' nine tails from a silver platter and hand it to the Abbess.

"Thank you, Sister Lizabet, you have chosen wisely." The merest hint of a smile flitted across the face of the Abbess; cruel or kind it was too quick for Olivia to tell. "Please bend over the rail."

The manner in which the nun obeyed suggested to Olivia that this was a ritual she was obliged to follow, and one she had evidently followed on a previous occasion. She knelt at the altar rail and leaned forward. It was low enough for her to bend right over, raising her bottom. When she had settled she shuffled her knees slightly apart. All seemed to be ready. A stir went through the congregation like a low humming of bees. Clearly the prospect of seeing their sister whipped was an exciting one.

"Her hair," said the Abbess, seemingly to nobody in particular. "Hold her hair."

One of her acolytes stepped beside the kneeling nun and lifted her long red hair from her back. She held it high, applying just enough tension to hold the head still; if she moved it would tug at the roots.

"Hands," the Abbess spoke again, and another acolyte tied the nun's outspread wrists to the altar rail with a cord. The cold-blooded manner of the preparation left Olivia shivering. Punishment in the House of Correction may have been crude, but it wasn't as sinister as this sickeningly efficient ritual.

The Abbess twirled the whip in her hand, fast enough to make the thongs hiss through the stifled atmosphere. Already the slim white buttocks clenched in fear.

"From this day on," the Abbess announced loudly and clearly, "you, Sister Lizabet, will willingly and graciously submit to whatever is required of you." The echo repeated from the high, vaulted roof. "You will obey every rule of this order. Further disobedience will not be tolerated. Brace yourself and make your confession to our patron saint." She held the whip high and raised her eyes to it in reverence. "This will teach you to never again deny us your body!" and the whip fell diagonally across the nun's back from shoulder to hip.

Her shriek filled the chapel with its deafening echo. Olivia quickly concluded that that was why it had been chosen in the first place; because of its capacity to exaggerate the suffering of the punished. By the time Olivia opened her eyes the whip had fallen again, in an opposite diagonal, producing the same pitiful screams. The weals were deeply etched in red and purple on the nun's pure back. The third stroke lashed her across the middle and she jolted at the rail.

"Hold the wretch," demanded the Abbess, her voice emphasizing total control of herself and those around her.

The acolyte tugged on the red hair and Olivia sympathized with the pain the girl must have felt. Her own scalp burned at the thought of what she was going through. The fourth stroke of the whip landed on the nun's vulnerable buttocks. The ends of the lashes whistled into her groin and the humming bees betrayed their approval. The poor nun writhed in pain and anguish.

Olivia could stand it no longer, she had to know what crime or transgression could possibly warrant such fearful retribution.

"She refused to obey," the nun beside her whispered in answer to her timid question.

"Obey what?"

"The rules of course. Everyone should obey the rules. Now be quiet - otherwise we'll both be in trouble as well."

"Tell me -" Olivia's voice raised a little and she quickly checked it, glancing around to make sure she hadn't been heard. "Please tell me what she's done wrong." The thigh pressed harder against hers, and she detected a quiver in the whisper that came close to her ear.

"She refused her lover the parting of her legs."

"Lover? I don't understand. Surely that's not permitted in a convent."

"Everything is permitted!" hissed Olivia's neighbour impatiently.

Because of their covert dialogue their heads were almost touching. Olivia suddenly became aware that she was being studied closely.

"My ... you are a pretty one," whispered the nun. "You're new here."

As Olivia blushed and nodded and tried to keep from looking at her neighbour a hand groped under her habit and rested on her thigh. It moved slowly back and forth, and then the fingers inched down towards her sex. "Am I supposed to permit this?" she breathed.

"Look at the altar rail and answer that for yourself."

Olivia didn't need to look; she could hear the screams coming from the nun and the harsh denunciations of the Abbess.

"It's an object lesson," the nun continued, her low voice thick with emotion, "the whip is enhancing pleasure after pain."

Olivia was thrown into confusion. She had suffered Rupert to give her a thrashing before taking her, but it had never been as brutal as this. And yet, paradoxically, the spectacle was highly arousing, and she could tell that everybody in the chapel found it highly arousing; not only the victim and the congregation, but the Abbess herself.

In the heat of the moment the sneaky nun had peeled open Olivia's sex and slipped her expert fingers inside. "Don't make a sound," she warned. "See how wet you already are."

Olivia was disgusted that she had been so aroused by such a dreadful exhibition. Shaken from the appalling sight going on at the altar she gripped the nun's forearm and forced the devious fingers away. To her surprise the nun did not object, but merely smiled and breathed huskily: "I will have you ... Sooner or later, I will have you." Olivia looked into the nun's confident eyes for the first time, and found little reason to disbelieve her words. She certainly did not relish the thought, but felt her nipples harden nonetheless. Thankfully her attention was wrenched back to the altar.

"See how she has learned her lesson," the Abbess addressed them all. The nun was released from the rail and pulled upright by her hair. She turned to face her sisters and Olivia nearly cried out from shock. Far from exhibiting a countenance seared with pain, she was savouring the throes of orgasm.

"Fix her with the collar," was the next command, and one of the acolytes opened an ornate casket. She took out a length of chain with an iron ring on the end and fitted it around the nun's neck. With the Abbess leading the procession, the acolyte pulled the nun after her, dragging her like a dog on a lead. As she passed along the aisle the congregation crowded forward to view her whipped back and bottom. Behind her followed the other acolyte, ceremonially flicking her back with the whip. They proceeded at a snail's pace, giving everyone ample opportunity to see at close quarters the livid stripes burning her skin. The procession continued all the way around the chapel until it arrived back where it had started, at the altar rail.

"Now will you submit?" the Abbess asked Sister Lizabet, who instantly nodded in return.

Olivia heard a shuffling behind her as another nun came out into the aisle. She advanced towards the altar rail, stripping off her habit as she went. She was completely naked when she got there.

Without warning the Abbess seized the whip and lashed her hinds as well.

"What on earth has she done?" Olivia dared to ask further.

"Nothing," came the blank reply. "She's her lover."

"The one she refused?"

Her informant nodded, keeping her eyes on what was taking place at the altar. The collar had been removed and the lovers had tumbled to the floor, rolling over and over and being whipped by the Abbess. Olivia couldn't deny the magnetism of her breasts which swayed enticingly beneath the black silk as she lashed into them. The vicious tails fell at random, striping buttocks, bellies, and thighs. Shrieks of delicious pain rose from the entwined couple as they locked their limbs in preparation for the final display.

"Are they really making love to each other?" Olivia gasped. The question needed no answer. Sister Lizabet lay on her back, thighs firmly wrapped around her partner. Her heels drummed into the small of her back. Her arms were around her shoulders, nails scoring into her spine.

All the while the Abbess continued to apply the whip, mainly on the thighs of Sister Lizabet. She squirmed as her flanks were striped by the tails. Her heels drummed faster. The Abbess switched her attention to the bare bottom of the lover, lashing into her cheeks with far greater gusto than she had previously. Olivia could see the effect that was having. Her bottom thrashed between Sister Lizabet's thighs until, with a wild shriek, she orgasmed. Sister Lizabet had already climaxed, her cries lost under the harsh cracks of the lash. They lay panting and gasping, still clutching each other, oblivious of the standing congregation watching their every move.

The Abbess seemed satisfied with their performance. "Go to the infirmary," she said, laying the whip neatly on the altar, "and see to yourselves. The rest of you, dismiss and be about your tasks."

The nuns filed decorously out of the chapel, dividing at the entrance and going off singly or in groups to different buildings that lined the walls. Olivia didn't know where to go. She wasn't going to be there for very long, another day or two at most, and from what she had seen that was a day or two too many. She headed back to her cell; a haven from this madhouse. She made up her mind to stay there until Flora had sent her money and clothes. Whatever took place in this convent - whippings and the most degrading exhibitions imaginable - it was no business of hers.

She crossed the courtyard and made her way up the stairs to her cell. The sound of the lash echoing in that chapel, with its filthy paintings and outrageous behaviour, was still ringing in her ears when she lifted the latch on the heavy cell door. "It's locked," she said aloud and stamped her foot.

"Of course it's locked. The cells are out of bounds during working hours."

Olivia spun round and saw a familiar face - one that was almost welcome. The handsome nun from the waggon smiled and took Olivia's hand.

"Where are you taking me?" she asked, letting herself be led along the passage to a shadowy flight of winding stone steps.

"To the Novitiate Mistress. We all have to be trained in the ways of the convent - it is the rules."

"But I don't want to be trained in the ways of the convent. I'm leaving here as soon as I can."

The nun ignored her every word and went on leading her up the cold steps until they reached a low door. She knocked, stooped, and went in. Behind a desk sat the Novitiate Mistress, scribbling in a ledger. She stood up when Olivia was presented to her.

"Thank you Sister Lupa, that will be all."

Sister Lupa bowed and left.

The Mistress looked like a school teacher with a pair of glasses perched on the end of her nose and her hair in a bun. Olivia could see that behind the austere appearance she was rather attractive. Her polite smile seemed relatively friendly.

"Welcome to the convent of saint Dulcinea," she said, having studied Olivia from head to toe over the top of her glasses. "I shall be taking care of you for the next week or so - just until you've settled in. Your name please."

"Mrs - I mean Miss - Olivia Holland, from London." Olivia decided to deal with the situation before matters got well and truly out of hand. "But there seems to have been a slight misunderstanding somewhere along the line; perhaps I should explain. You see, I'm only here for a day or so until some money and clothes arrive from my friend. Then I'll be leaving for Ottery. In fact, I was going to ask if I could send a telegram." She judged a little diplomacy would be prudent. "I must say, however, that I am exceedingly grateful for all the kindness shown to me since your Sisters found me on the road."

"You are welcome, Miss Holland. And you've no need to worry about your friend - we've already sent a telegram."

"You have?"

The Mistress shifted uncomfortably and looked a little annoyed with herself. "Yes ... one of our Sisters knew of a Flora, who runs a boarding-house in Ottery."

"Oh - I see."

"In the meantime," the Mistress quickly changed the subject, "we do have a slight problem. That is to say, well ... how can I put this ..." A stern expression creased her brow as she impatiently checked a few pages of the ledger.

"Look, if I can help you in any way," Olivia offered, hoping to conclude this unsettling meeting quickly.

"Well, yes Miss Holland, you could help." Her widening smile for some reason made Olivia think of a fox. "It's just a silly old tradition really. You know how these things seem to hang on over the years. An examination - just for the records, you understand. I shall get into trouble if I don't carry it out."

"What do you mean - a medical examination?"

The Mistress clasped her hands together atop the ledger, a satisfied look on her face. "I knew a young woman of your obvious intelligence would understand. It really is no more than a formality. Is that acceptable?"

Olivia considered her predicament for a moment, and decided it would certainly be wiser to conform with these women. "Yes - I suppose so."

"Excellent," gushed the Mistress. "Would you remove your habit then, please Miss Holland, and step onto those," she indicated a set of weighing scales.

The image of Sister Lizabet being whipped flashed

through Olivia's mind. She hesitated for a moment, and then undressed and stepped onto the scales. The Mistress stood and balanced an iron weight on the other end and read the result off a dial.

"Eight stone. Hmmm, a little underweight for a young lady of your height."

"Five feet and ten inches," Olivia confirmed.

"And very healthy with it, no doubt."

The Mistress shuffled a little closer and patted Olivia's bottom. "Nice and firm around here," she muttered. "What about up top?" She felt Olivia's breasts, squeezing them and running her fingers over the nipples. "Nice and firm here too. Would you open your legs, please."

Olivia was tempted to question the reasons for such an eccentric examination, but she held her tongue and slid her feet apart. A cold hand immediately nudged between her legs, rubbing softly to and fro. Olivia closed her eyes and felt her cheeks tingle at the shock of the intimate touch.

"Now," the Mistress continued mumbling, apparently unaware of the effect her fingers were having on the young lady before her. "Let's have a look at your legs." She stooped a little. "No problems there I see. Thighs nice and sturdy ... likewise the calves." Finally she placed a palm on Olivia's ribs and felt for the heartbeat. "Strong as a horse, if you'll pardon the expression."

Olivia was indeed beginning to feel a little like an animal for sale at the market. "Can I put my clothes back on now, please?"

"Not just yet, I still have one other little thing left to do. A test of strength, so to speak."

"What sort of a test?" Olivia asked uneasily.

"It's another tradition the Abbess insists upon," the Mistress answered. "Personally, I'd dispense with all these rituals and just get on with it."

"Get on with what?" Olivia didn't like the way this was developing.

"Life of course. A healthy young lady like you is quite capable of dealing with anything that's thrown at her. I can see that." Her smile unsettled Olivia even more. "Still, we have to do these things."

She went back to the ledger, and was soon so absorbed in recording Olivia's details that she seemed to have forgotten her.

"About this test," Olivia prompted, somewhat timidly.

The Mistress looked up. "Oh yes, I'd forget my head if … Go along the passage and through the door at the end. I'll be with you as soon as you're ready."

"Ready?"

"My assistants will show you what's required."

"When this examination is over," Olivia ventured to ask, "will someone please try to make further contact with my friend to find out when my things will arrive."

"As soon as we've done," the Mistress smiled.

Olivia left the room and walked further along the gloomy passage. She wasn't happy with events, but was eager to get this over with. She found the door at the end, took a deep breath, and went in. There was nothing much to see, except lots of rusty chains hanging from the walls and an old rocking-horse. She jumped a little when she first noticed the three nuns sitting quietly in the half-light, evidently awaiting her arrival. Their faces were in shadow, but she assumed they were watching her. Her nerves began to feel somewhat frayed.

"I - I was told to report here," she broke the silence. "For a test of some sort."

Two nuns stood and silently approached. One of them patted the saddle of the rocking-horse. "Up you come then," whispered the other one.

Olivia sighed with a growing sense of annoyance. She couldn't see the point of these silly rituals, particularly as they didn't really apply to her because she would soon be leaving for Ottery.

She studied the horse, and noted it was not of the rocking variety after all, but stood on a centre column of iron. It was much larger than any she'd seen before, and when she put her foot in the stirrup the nuns had to help her swing over the saddle. Olivia wondered if they really had to touch her bottom quite so intimately in doing so. She looked at the floor; now she was up it seemed a long way down. Instead of reins the horse was fitted with chains that ended with rings. She reached forward and took them in her hands, assuming that to be the correct thing to do.

"Not like that," said one nun quietly, and gently fastened the rings around Olivia's wrists. "Now your feet."

The calm disposition of the two assistants relaxed Olivia just a little, and she made no move to resist. She obediently slid her feet further into the stirrups and the nun clamped them with an iron hasp. Her legs were almost straight, and when she tried to move she found her bottom could only lift a couple of inches off the saddle. "Am I ready now?" she asked.

Neither of the assistants answered, but the silence was broken by echoing footsteps approaching the room. The door creaked open and the Mistress entered holding some sort of heavy handle and her ledger. She passed the handle to one of the nuns, and told her to wind up the 'old devil'. Olivia was feeling apprehensive. The handle was inserted under the horse's belly and clunked as it struggled to turn. Together the two assistants strained and grunted to wind it fully. While they laboured and sweated beneath the beast the Mistress inspected Olivia's wrists and ankles, making sure they were firmly secured.

"We don't want you falling off," she muttered, "now do we?"

Olivia didn't know how to reply.

The handle was removed from its socket and a lever protruding from the horse's side was pulled by the Mistress. It moved easily, and a grinding and grating of metal started up inside the beast. Olivia clung to the chains expecting the whole contraption to start rocking to and fro, but nothing seemed to happen. They all waited in silence, and Olivia was about to request they release her when she felt a slight movement between her buttocks; a gentle nudge of something cold. Whatever it was prodded again and tentatively probed her sex. Olivia gasped with shock. The mystery object felt round and smooth.

"What are you doing to me?" she pleaded.

"Do not resist it," murmured the Mistress, stroking her thigh soothingly. "It'll be better for you if you do not resist it."

Olivia tried to relax, and instantly caught her breath. The object rising from the saddle was long and cylindrical. "Oh no ..." she wailed softly. "Why are you doing this to me? Please stop."

The Mistress reached up and dabbed Olivia's perspiring brow. "We can't stop the engine until the spring has run its course."

The phallus rose steadily higher. "I can't take this," Olivia moaned.

"I'm sure you can," encouraged the Mistress softly, "a healthy young lady like you."

Olivia knew there was to be no reprieve. She gingerly settled her bottom on the saddle, feeling the rude object force even deeper. She closed her eyes and filled her lungs, feeling one of the silent observers - probably the Mistress - cupping her heaving breasts. Despite her dismay she shuddered from the breathless cocktail of trepidation and mounting pleasure. Being so obviously the centre of attention in the still room somehow added to her excitement.

"Magnificent ..."

Through swirling emotions Olivia heard the whispered compliment and a quill scratching across paper, but those distractions did little to dampen her shameful enjoyment.

Fingers delved between her hot thighs. "She's taken it all," confirmed one of the nuns.

The phallus vibrated in Olivia's clutching vagina. She gripped the chains and instinctively rode the magnificent machine, rocking backwards and forwards and rising and falling as much as her bonds would allow.

"The young lady learns quickly," observed the Mistress approvingly.

Perspiration coated Olivia's breasts and gathered in her deep cleavage. Her whole body glistened from her exertions, and was growing heavy with exhaustion. Her back arched and her mouth gaped. As the machine slowed and the vibrator stopped she groaned loudly and came. The beast stilled, and Olivia slumped forward over its neck, her chained arms swaying limply.

The Mistress scrawled a final note in her ledger, underlined it with a flourish, and then turned to the two nuns. "Thank you both for your assistance."

They bowed and retook their seats as the third nun rose and glided forward. The Mistress smiled at her from behind the glasses with a glint in her eyes that suggested more than just courtesy. "Have you been paid, Sister Letitia?"

"I am owed for the room at the White Garter, and for the oaf at the cottage. He was greedy, and demanded more than we'd bargained for."

"But you paid?"

"I took the decision to meet his demands, yes."

The Mistress reached out and touched Sister Letitia's hand. "You did well, my dear. How much are you owed?"

"Ten shillings in all, Mistress."

"Then you may go to the treasury and collect it."

"Thank you, Mistress. And what shall we do with Miss Holland?"

"Have her taken to her cell and washed. Give her a sleeping draft and put her to bed. I think she's earned that much."

CHAPTER SEVEN

Olivia awoke as she had slept; with her fingers subconsciously working to resurrect the ghost of the orgasm that had so aroused her on the iron horse.

"Good morning, miss."

Olivia blushed and hastily snatched the blanket up under her chin as a cheerful nun swept into her cell and opened the shutters.

"It's a lovely day," the newcomer beamed.

The tiny cell flooded with light. The nun placed a bowl of porridge and a jug of milk on the old table.

This was only Olivia's second morning in the convent, yet somehow she felt as if she had been there for weeks. She was not so much a guest - she was more of an inmate. She was sure there was a pattern to all this. "I wish to speak to the Abbess," she said, picking her habit up from the floor beside her cot.

The nun poured her a beaker of milk. "Why should you want to do that? The Abbess sees only those she wishes to see."

"I want to see her immediately. I shall be leaving today, with or without her permission."

"Perhaps you should speak to the Novitiate Mistress first. I'm sure she could help you."

"I don't want to see the Novitiate Mistress," Olivia retorted, feeling a little more confident with the dawn of a new day. "I want to see the Abbess."

"But why? You've passed your initiation."

Olivia did not care for that remark; an initiation usually meant the beginning of things to come, and she had no desire to discover what those things might be.

"I would like you to take me to her … please."

"I can't."

"Why?" asked Olivia desperately.

"Because she'll be taking mass in a few minutes. You'd better hurry - we've all got to be there. I'm on my way to the chapel now."

"But -" Before Olivia could explain that she had nothing to do with the convent and their daily rituals the chirpy nun had turned with a flurry and a swish of her habit and was gone. Olivia groaned, but sat at the table and ate the porridge; it was her intention to leave today for Ottery, whatever anybody else might say, and so she would need as much fuel as possible. Once she had scraped the bowl clean she decided to go to the chapel to have it out with the Abbess.

The chapel … now where was that?

Down the stairs and across the courtyard. Olivia could hear the bell tolling - its eerie tone sent a chill right through her. She reached the bottom of the stairs and came to a curious dead end; a blank wall of stone. She cursed, retraced her steps, and went along another corridor.

She tried a door with large iron hinges, and found herself in a depressing and musty scriptorium. Books lay open on the desks, and her natural curiosity made her look and flick over some pages. They were magnificently illustrated manuscripts glowing with colour, and all of them full of the most incredible pictures she had ever seen. Her mind went back to the chapel, to the painting over the chancel arch. She suddenly felt as if she'd been transported back in time, to an age long dead when torture and the violation of women were an everyday occurrence. The books seemed to be instruction manuals of some sort, written in gothic script that she couldn't understand. Strange symbols and codes littered the pages, along with paintings of men and women suffering flagellation and various other ordeals. She had forgotten about the Abbess; the fascinating books gripped her.

The largest tome was almost as big as the desktop. Olivia struggled to open it. What she saw took her breath away. There was a wheel divided into sections, each with a picture, and at the centre was a painting of a figure - half man and half woman. The paintings in the segments were of men and women indulging in sexual intercourse, and every one of them was flogging the other. Some with whips, others with rods, but the expressions were identical; pure, unadulterated ecstasy. Olivia shuddered, but could not tear her eyes away.

Her finger traced the perimeter of the wheel where more figures romped through the air in wild abandon, headed by a splendidly painted woman riding a broomstick. Her long legs were thrown outwards so that the reader could see her minutely executed sex. There was no doubt that the broomstick was a substitute for a man's organ. The look on her face told Olivia she was at the height of orgasm. Presumably the symbols and zodiacal codes referred to the woman herself. Olivia managed to close the huge book with a dull thump. She fanned away the rising dust and read the cover inscription: *Sanctus Licentia Copulatum*.

"I wonder what it means," she said aloud.

"It means, mind your own business."

"Oh!" Olivia spun round, her heart pounding in her chest. A pair of glasses flashed at her. The Mistress pounced with surprising agility, grabbed her arms and shook her.

"Let go!" Olivia wailed. "Please - you're hurting me!"

"You were coming along so nicely," the Mistress hissed into her face. "You passed your initiation far better than most. I had such high hopes of you. And now what do I find? Here you are in our beloved scriptorium violating the sacred books! You're a harlot! You'll be severely punished for this gross act!"

She shook the poor girl all the more.

"Let me go! I didn't mean to do any wrong! Please - I was just looking for the Abbess to tell her I'll be leaving today! I want to make my way to Ottery - if you could arrange a little food and some clothes. Ouch! You're hurting me!"

The Mistress was unrelenting. A little spittle landed on Olivia's cheek as she spat: "The only arrangement I'm going to make is for your trip to the punishment chamber!"

Olivia caught hold of the desk and hung on for dear life. The Mistress pinched her upper arms in a vice-like grip and tugged in the opposite direction.

"No! Let go of me!" begged Olivia.

"You let go of that desk! Do as I tell you!"

"Please, I want to see the Abbess!"

Both females were panting and heaving as they pulled to and fro. A stack of four large volumes wobbled precariously on the corner of the desk, and as Olivia's hip slammed against the wooden edge they toppled onto the floor with a loud thump, and lay in twisted and folded disarray.

"Look what you've done, you slut!"

"I'm sorry!" protested Olivia.

"No one sees the Abbess - except by invitation! It's one of the rules!" The Mistress prepared for one last haul to dislodge the little vixen from the desk.

"But I'm not part of your rules!" Olivia anticipated the final assault and let go of the sturdy furniture. With a shriek and a flurry of limbs they both toppled to the stone floor. The older woman's glasses flew off her nose and Olivia kicked them under the desk. While the Mistress floundered about in search of them Olivia nimbly jumped to her feet and bolted through the nearest door. She found herself in another cold corridor with more doors leading off it. The whole horrible place was a labyrinth of passages and flights of echoing steps. Olivia's instincts told her to head for the chapel where the Abbess was certain to be; but how to get there? She descended some steps. They kept taking her down. She considered going back, but the Mistress would be waiting, and besides, she would surely reach the bottom soon. The walls became darker and more grimy as she descended. Underfoot the steps were slippery with mould. Water dripped and echoed from the ghostly shadows. She must have gone too far. Her senses told her she was underground.

She eventually, and with not a little relief, reached a passageway. The only faint shafts of light came from gratings overhead. At the end of the passage she found a door. It was so small she had to stoop low to pass through. As she straightened and peered around the room in which she found herself the door slammed behind her.

"Now," said the Mistress, "if you have finished your fun and games, we can get on with the tiresome business of teaching you some manners."

Olivia was speechless. She backed away from the Mistress. There was only one door into the room, the one she had just come through, and it would have been impossible for the Mistress to have overtaken her between the scriptorium and here. "But - but how did you get here ahead of me?" she blurted.

"You have much to learn, Miss Holland. Finding your way around the convent is only one of them. Learning not to go poking about in things that do not concern you is another. Now, kindly take off your habit."

Olivia had a snap decision to make. She could show defiance, and risk making things worse for herself, and perhaps even find herself imprisoned, or she could comply and hope to appeal to the compassionate side of these women and maybe even find an opportunity to escape. She decided the latter course would be the more prudent. "Is this another of your strange rituals?" she asked meekly as she pulled the habit over her head.

"Do not question my religion." There was no longer anger in her tone.

"What sort of religion is this?"

"That's what I'm here to teach you."

"I don't want to be taught anything. I'd rather go and see the Abbess."

"She won't see you, so please do as I say." The Mistress took off her glasses and wiped them on a handkerchief, before balancing them on the end of her nose once again. She patted her bun and smoothed down her habit. Everything she did was studied, as precise as the workings of a watch. Her movements were smooth and her air authoritative, and Olivia found herself relaxing slightly.

"Stand in the middle of the floor, Miss Holland, and put your right hand out in front of you."

Olivia obeyed.

"Thank you."

A chain that Olivia hadn't before paid any attention to

hung from the ceiling just above her. The Mistress reached up, pulled it down, and fitted the manacle at its end around the tentatively offered wrist. She locked it and then put the key in her pocket. Leaving Olivia for a moment, she went to a corner of the small room and huddled over. Olivia tugged experimentally on the chain and her wary eyes followed its course up to the ceiling where it passed over a pulley and then down to a drum where it wrapped round and round. On the drum was a handle which the Mistress began to slowly turn, drawing the chain through the pulley and lifting Olivia's hand high above her head until her arm was fully stretched and she was straining uncomfortably on tiptoe. When satisfied, the Mistress locked the handle with a peg so it couldn't unwind.

"Ooh, please," Olivia sobbed. "You're hurting me."

The Mistress checked her handiwork with the satisfied look of an expert who knows she's done her work well. "Stop complaining. A little time alone to consider your misdeeds will do you nothing but good."

"But -"

"I'm just going to tidy the scriptorium, after your silly little tantrum just now."

"But you can't leave me here like this!"

The door slammed and Olivia was left alone in the cold and gloomy silence. The manacle cut into her wrist and her calves already burned.

"Please! Come back! Don't leave me!"

The pain spread excruciatingly through her body. It crept up her calves and thighs, burned its way through her tensed buttocks, and up her arched spine. There it fused with the agony numbing her shoulders and back. How long would she be left like this? Whatever happened, she must not lose consciousness ...

"Well now, let's have a look at you."

Olivia's head stirred from her chest. Her whole body was numb. She watched drowsily the Mistress pat and stroke her thighs, feeling the tension in her iron-hard muscles.

"We shall have to do something to ease your discomfort," Olivia heard, and then felt a soothing ointment being massaged into her stiff limbs. "Does that feel better?"

"Yes," Olivia managed. "Thank you." She was feeling confused by the two contrasting moods of cruelty and kindness shown by the Mistress. The fingertips rubbing in gentle circles against her temples felt good.

"I must soon take you to the punishment chamber."

"Must you?"

"Yes," said the Mistress firmly. "You were wrong to enter the scriptorium, and having violated our sacred place your behaviour was then quite unforgivable. You must therefore suffer the consequences."

Olivia whimpered. "Please let me down."

"You are a disobedient young lady," the Mistress continued. "And disobedience will not be tolerated."

"I didn't want to come here," protested Olivia. "I wouldn't have if I hadn't been in such need."

"Clearly your need is for correction." The Mistress licked her lips with a strange look in her eyes. She held Olivia around the waist and reached up to unlock the manacle. "But first we'll just get your blood flowing again."

The manacle sprang open and Olivia slumped against the warmth of the nun. Her arm flopped uselessly and her legs failed her. The Mistress lowered her to the dusty floor, knelt beside her and cradled her in her arms. Olivia buried her face into the safety of the dark habit.

"There, there, child - no need for tears. Once they've finished with you in the punishment chamber I shall see that you are taken to the infirmary. There the herbalist will take good care of you."

"Why am I being treated like this?" Olivia sobbed. "I thought convents were supposed to be places of sanctuary, and that nuns are kind and gentle souls, devoted to prayer. But so far I've seen in this place nothing but cruelty."

"True, but the cruelty is not without purpose. Look upon each punishment you undergo as a step closer to the completion of your Novitiate. Your submission to the whip and your survival of it will prove you are worthy of admission."

"Admission to what?"

"Why, to our order of course. It is a privilege granted only to the lucky few."

"But I don't want to join your order. I want to go -"

"Enough of this." There was sufficient threat in the tone of the Mistress for Olivia to take heed. "Cease your foolish chatter and rest awhile."

She cradled Olivia's head into her breasts, and Olivia allowed the reassuring closeness to ease her anguish. Her limbs were rapidly recovering, and she slowly began to feel better. She closed her eyes and enjoyed the fingers stroking her brow. Material rustled. Olivia felt soft flesh against her cheek, and breathed the delicate scent of the Mistress. A hand cupped the back of her head and guided it down until a nipple brushed across her lips. She willingly opened her mouth and sucked as the erect bud was fed inside. She heard a soft moan and the nipple twitched as she gently grazed it with her teeth.

"Suck me," the Mistress whispered. "My breast will soothe away all your troubles."

It was true; the nipple seemed to bring a restfulness she had not known for a long while. Her body relaxed totally as the Mistress rocked gently back and forth.

"Oh yes, my little one," she purred. "That's right, suck me. Suck as hard as you like. Soothe away your troubles."

The nipple pulsed between Olivia's lips as she sucked hungrily. The whole breast quivered. Olivia could feel and hear the nun's heart pounding. Her breathing became deeper. Her chest rose and fell in a steady and rhythmic swell against her cheek.

"Oh that's beautiful. Go on, my little one. Don't stop. Oh, oh, yesss ..." The Mistress choked back a sob and clutched Olivia's head ever closer to her breast.

Excitement was awakening in the pit of Olivia's stomach too. It was impossible to ignore the huskily aroused voice close to her ear, and the delicious nipple in her mouth. She couldn't resist cupping the firm breast and giving it a gentle squeeze. The Mistress responded with a plaintive cry and slipped a hand between Olivia's legs. "Oh, you're so wet," she panted. "I can feel how wet you are." Her accomplished fingers slipped to and fro across Olivia's labia, coaxing forth her juices and making them flow. Olivia moaned and sucked even harder on the nipple, devouring as much of the breast as she could.

"Yes, just like that," the Mistress encouraged. "That feels *so* good. You're *very* clever."

Olivia suckled like a child. The gentle coaxing of the Mistress and the clever fingers between her legs fueled her own mounting pleasure. "Oh," the nipple plopped from between her succulent lips. "I'm coming."

The Mistress shuddered and fed her other breast into Olivia's willing mouth. "You mustn't come yet," she moaned, running her trembling fingers through Olivia's tumbling hair.

"I - I'll try not to," she managed to mumble around the nipple.

They were suddenly all fingers and tongues, frantically

sucking and probing at each other. Their juices flowed. Olivia fumbled and searched beneath the black habit and rubbed between the older woman's thighs. She felt beautifully lightheaded; warm and safe.

"It always makes me feel like this," panted the Mistress. Suddenly her whole body gave a colossal shudder. Her arms and legs went rigid as she reached her orgasm. She threw back her head and cried with delight. Olivia followed her with a subdued whimper and slumped against her bosom, her head buried in the sweet smelling cleavage.

"Leave your hand where it is," the Mistress told her when she started to withdraw.

Olivia obeyed, feeling too mellow to do otherwise. The Mistress returned the compliment, and together they remained locked in fond embrace, quietly moving their fingers to and fro, prolonging each other's pleasure.

"Was that part of your rituals?" Olivia whispered sweetly.

The Mistress stroked her hair affectionately. "Shhh, rest awhile. Soon I shall have to take you to the punishment chamber."

"Do you really have to? Couldn't I stay with you? I don't want to be punished."

"That's impossible."

Olivia looked up into her eyes. "Why?"

"Because I have to do my duty and see that you receive your correction." Her voice seemed genuinely sad, the words spoken reluctantly.

"Do I really deserve to be punished?"

"You do. And if the Abbess discovered you had not received the appropriate chastisement she would have me take your place, and I would suffer much more severely then you ever will."

"Perhaps if I spoke to her and explained," Olivia offered optimistically.

"There is nothing to explain. You were caught in the scriptorium, and that is enough. If she learned that you also defied me the punishment would be much worse."

"So I am to be whipped, like that nun in the chapel?"

The Mistress went strangely quiet before answering. "You are."

Olivia could sense the disconcerting mood returning to the cold room. The fingers disappeared from between her legs. "Who will punish me?" she asked fearfully.

"That is not for me to say." The Mistress stood and straightened her habit; her composure and air of authority restored. "Come along," she said tartly, "they're waiting."

Olivia rose and put her habit back on. She was suddenly filled with resolve. Tomorrow would be her third day in this place, and she made up her mind it would definitely be her last. She would let these spiteful women whip her if they must; it would probably be no worse than she had experienced before; a vindictive warning not to go nosing in places where she had no business. They could keep their silly old books and weird paintings. Olivia had an idea. "Do you promise to see they take me to the infirmary afterwards?" she asked.

The Mistress nodded. "I promise."

Olivia brightened a little; some time in the infirmary would give her a chance to devise an escape. Already a plan was forming in her head. It would come to fruition while she lay quietly in her bed. Hospitals were ideal places to bide ones time. She had done that in the House of Correction; stalling, pretending to be much sicker than she really was.

"Then I am ready." She took a deep breath and moved toward the door like a convicted criminal taking her last walk to the gallows.

CHAPTER EIGHT

The punishment chamber was a dank, subterranean dungeon with chains hanging from the ceiling. The walls were of plaster with the fragments of crumbling paintings peeling from them. Some half-hearted attempts had been made to restore them, but had been abandoned. A more successful restoration had been completed on the ceiling. Olivia took it in with a sweeping glance; a woman, seemingly falling from a starry sky. Quite startling in its way.

Four nuns stood along one wall facing her as she in turn was positioned in the centre of the chamber. One second The Mistress was standing on Olivia's shoulder announcing her presence, and the next second she was gone. Olivia swiveled around to see where she was, but there was no sign of her ever having been there.

The four nuns were not dressed in their usual habits, but wore thin tunics of pale yellow cotton which just reached down to mid-thigh. They apparently wore nothing underneath, and Olivia could clearly see the outline of their voluptuous figures. The tunics had been designed to draw attention to the more obvious aspects of their bodies; dark pubic triangles and nipples showed through the shimmering cotton.

But it was not that which arrested Olivia's eyes, it was the serpents embroidered on the tunics. They coiled around the nuns and finished with their heads pointing down over their bellies. The red forked tongues licked between their thighs; there was lecherous intent in the serpents' slanting eyes. As the nuns advanced upon Olivia the images came alive, the coils wriggling over their hips and breasts and the heads diving between their legs.

Olivia stood mesmerized.

"Strip yourself."

She looked up and gasped with shock. "You? But how?"

Sister Letitia reached out and gripped the front of Olivia's habit. One vicious tear ripped it from her body. "I am very pleased to make your acquaintance ... again," she smiled. "You've certainly led us a merry dance, fighting with the Mistress like a street ruffian and prying into the sacred books. Now you must pay for your indiscretions."

"You never told me you're a nun," Olivia said, somewhat bemused. "Why didn't you tell me?"

"You never asked." The four nuns chuckled smugly.

"But you directed me to that disgraceful hovel called an inn! Why did you do that?"

Sister Letitia looked a little impatient. "Because it's the kind of place you said you were looking for ... Lots of men, remember?" The nuns chuckled again and Olivia blushed bright scarlet at the reminder. "Besides, it was all part of the plan."

"Plan? What plan? Why have you tricked me? For you surely have!"

"Would you have come here of your own accord?"

"No - I wouldn't set foot inside the place if you paid me."

"Well you have set foot inside the place, and we haven't paid you. You came here voluntarily, seeking rest and shelter. And while you are here, you will abide by our rules."

"What are these rules?" Olivia wailed with exasperation.

"I don't understand at all. I think you make them up as you go along. It's just an excuse to torment me. All these absurd rituals I have to go through -"

"Those *absurd* rituals have been practiced since time began. They are there for the guidance of the wise and the obedience of the willful. You are both disobedient and willful. The more willful you are, the harsher the punishment. You were only to receive a flogging, but under the circumstances we think you ought to be racked into the bargain."

"I am not disobedient," Olivia protested. "I'll obey any rules you like. If only I knew what they were."

"Well, now you will learn. Sisters, will you please prepare Olivia whilst I consult the punishment book."

Sister Letitia went to a lectern in one corner, opened the appropriate volume, and read the gothic text and perused a gorgeously hand-painted illustration. The three other nuns held Olivia tight.

"In accordance with the advice before me, you are to receive twelve lashes on your front, and a further twelve on your back. In addition you should receive twenty-four turns of the screws - but I will make allowances. You shall receive half that number if you promise to obey forthwith, without question, without a murmur of dissent."

Olivia listened open-mouthed as Sister Letitia finished announcing the sentence. She felt irons being fitted to her wrists behind her back, but was too dumbstruck to object. Her ankles were secured similarly. If acceptance meant the punishment would be over in half the time, then so be it. She would accept anything to be rid of this chamber and its foul occupants. She could then go to the infirmary and stay there until help arrived. Flora would rescue her. It would take more than the bespectacled Mistress and her loathsome minions to stop Flora once her fury was roused!

"Good," said Sister Letitia, closing the huge book and interpreting Olivia's silence as capitulation. "Sister Alysoun, will you put the willful Miss Holland on the rack while I decide which instrument I shall use."

The rack looked for all the world like a bed stripped of its sheets and blankets. The stout wooden framework had rungs across its width. At each end were rollers with levers. A complicated system of cogs and ratchets could just be glimpsed at the base of each lever.

"Lie face down," Sister Alysoun told her abruptly.

Olivia studied the contraption with dread, wondering what evil genius had dreamt up its design. It appeared to be very old; it's timbers were blackened with age and the cogs were wooden instead of metal. "Can we not sort out this misunderstanding some other way?" she tried to appeal to their better natures one last time - although she seriously doubted they had better natures. "I've already promised to be obedient. Surely that's enough."

"Then be obedient now and do as I say," said Sister Alysoun.

"I'm going to speak to the Abbess about this," she grumbled, crawling onto the monstrosity. She tried to get comfortable, but a rung flattened her breasts and others jutted painfully against her hips and knees.

"Arms," Sister Alysoun continued her orders. "Put them above your head."

Olivia obeyed. The manacles were fastened to two lengths of rope coming from the roller.

"Feet," said a dark-skinned nun with flashing eyes, and she secured Olivia's ankles to the roller at the foot of the rack in the same manner as her wrists. Then they took up their stations beside their respective rollers. At that moment Sister Letitia returned holding a forked whip, knotted at intervals along its leather thongs.

"Oh please," Olivia strained to see over her shoulder and whimpered. "You'll kill me with that!"

Sister Letitia cracked the weapon through the stagnant air. "I doubt that very much - but you will have a very sore bottom. I can guarantee that."

"May we change places?" the dark-skinned nun asked Sister Alysoun. "I'd like to see how much she can take of this."

Sister Alysoun looked to Sister Letitia, Sister Letitia nodded her consent, and the two nuns exchanged positions. There was a definite pecking-order in this place, and Olivia wondered for a moment what someone of Sister Letitia's tender years could have done to gain such a position of authority.

"Sister Walpurga," Sister Letitia signaled the commencement of the punishment, "you may begin."

The dark-skinned nun took up the strain and wrenched on her lever. Olivia's arms were drawn towards the roller. The rack was of such a length that even with her arms and legs at full stretch they would not touch the rollers.

"And now Sister Alysoun."

Olivia heard the ratchet and her legs were tugged completely straight. All at once her suspicions toward the gruesome appliance were realized. She had seen one similar in the Tower of London on a visit with Rupert one wet Sunday afternoon. The man being stretched was only a wax dummy, but the look of unremitting agony on his face had been real enough. Now it was going to happen to her, not as an attraction for those macabre members of the general public, but for real. The nuns were going to stretch her from finger to toe. "You can't do this to me!" she bawled. "This is disgraceful!"

The levers merely clicked against the wooden cogs, increasing the tension in her limbs.

"We can do this," Sister Letitia told her. "It's written in the sacred books. Racking and whipping are perfectly legal, providing the rules are properly followed."

What were the rules? Something set down in the middle-ages when this sort of thing was accepted as quite normal? What else did the rules say? That her tormentors would turn each lever a cog at a time, stretching her limbs slowly so she would feel every twinge of pain. They would go on levering until her body lifted from the frame, stretched to its fullest extent, arms and legs tearing from their sockets. Then what? Whip her until she fainted. No wonder the Novitiate Mistress had booked her a bed at the infirmary. There would be no reason to fake anything. Her suffering would be real.

Sister Walpurga placed her foot on the edge of the frame for better purchase. The muscles in her thigh hardened, her splendid calf knotted as she clicked the lever against the cog. Olivia heard Walpurga grunt with the effort, and looked up into the flashing eyes where she saw nothing but sadistic lust. She would not give this creature from the dark ages the satisfaction of hearing her beg for mercy. She would not be defeated!

The levers were pulled in opposite directions, the ratchets clicked, and slowly, very slowly, her arms and legs were lifted off the rungs. The pressure on her breasts, hips and knees gradually lessened. But that small relief was short-lived. Suddenly the ropes yanked her whole poor body right off the frame. She gritted her teeth against the searing pain tearing through her hips and shoulders. The tips of her nipples swayed just above the wooden rungs. Her legs and arms were fore and aft, as straight as tent poles. She felt like a length of knicker elastic stretched to the point of snapping.

"Ten lashes on your back and bottom, Miss Holland,"

Sister Letitia repeated the punishment superciliously. "And a further ten on your front."

Walpurga expressed her dissatisfaction at the 'leniency' in no uncertain terms, claiming she should receive at least double the dosage. But Sister Letitia overruled her. For once Olivia was grateful she was so punctilious.

Not to be outdone Walpurga grabbed her hair and forced a strip of tanned leather between her teeth. "Bite on this, it might help." She sniggered. "It might - but I doubt it."

The knotted thongs whipped viciously across Olivia's bottom. They were long enough to coil and bite around her rigid form. She spasmed against the restraints and howled into the gag.

"She squeals like a stuck hog!" spat Walpurga with contempt.

"Silence," demanded Sister Letitia. "I need to concentrate on my task. It must be carried out in accordance with the sacred book."

Walpurga sulked. From the corner of her fearful eye Olivia saw her kneel beside the rack. She feared the powerful dark-skinned beauty almost as much as the whip. When the leather hissed and struck again Walpurga reached forward and squeezed Olivia's jolting breasts.

"Your tits swing like the bells," Walpurga whispered crudely.

Olivia shuddered at the cold touch. As Sister Letitia continued to apply the lash, striking further and further up her back, the calculating hands squeezed harder and harder. She wasn't sure where the pain was most acute; in her whipped flanks and bottom, or her crushed breasts.

"Your tits look good enough to eat," Walpurga goaded. She might have even attempted to match deed to word if Sister Letitia had not ordered the slackening of the ropes. Olivia's body hit the rungs with a thud, and she uttered a long, tired groan.

"Put her on her back," the orders continued.

The ropes were released from the iron rings and the nun who had not yet taken any part in the proceedings bent over the frame. She went about her task quickly. Her arms went under Olivia, and with surprising dexterity she flipped her over.

Olivia whimpered; the rungs dug into her whipped back and buttocks as she was re-tethered. The ropes were pulled tight and she soon bridged the rack again.

Sister Letitia looked down at the taut limbs. It was a body that could have been created solely for the purpose of giving pleasure. Running her hands over it was too much to resist. She felt the thighs, the splendid strength in their long, creamy expanse. She felt the hollow of the stomach. She felt the ribs protruding in magnificent symmetry. She felt the flattened breasts which stretched up to the shoulders, which themselves had narrowed into the sides of the swan-neck.

"She is beautiful," Sister Alysoun broke the silence.

"Indeed," Sister Letitia mused.

Walpurga experienced a moment of jealousy. She too appreciated beauty when she saw it, but not in the way of the others. It was not there to be admired like a work of art, but to be enjoyed, physically. She would seize her moment. She would have to get there before her rivals. Already, in her minds eye, Olivia was writhing in her arms.

Olivia stared at the ceiling, away from the victorious eyes of her tormentors; she had seen that consuming look in the eyes of those who had punished her in the House of Correction. She shivered inside.

The attendant nuns stepped clear of the frame as Letitia gathered the whip. It slashed down, welting her from hip to breast, a diagonal stripe of excruciating pain. The next struck the tops of her thighs. The lashes snapped around them. There was no part of her that would be spared. Her body, back and front, would be welted from the coiling thongs. The knots would embed themselves at will, stinging where they struck. She saw the weapon whistle over Sister Letitia's shoulder and felt the burning pain branding her belly. Her insides were on fire, a blazing furnace roaring at the most sensual part of her being. She knew she was losing control of her senses, being overwhelmed by the agony churning in her belly.

"The ceiling ..." Sister Alysoun's voice prompted from somewhere. "Look at the ceiling ..."

It was as if she were gazing into a starry sky. Hundreds of glittering stars beamed down from the void, but it was the painting of the beautiful woman that possessed her. She seemed to be swooping down towards her. The shapely arms were outstretched as if hurrying into a long awaited embrace. Olivia stared into the startling eyes which bore into her own. They were only paint on plaster, but flashed as real as Walpurga's.

Suddenly the ordeal was over. The levers creaked once again. The cogs turned one tooth at a time and Olivia was no longer suspended by her aching limbs. The manacles were removed, but the pain did not go away. Every muscle that had been stretched or whipped shrieked in agony.

The quiet nun brought a pail of water and a cloth. As she removed the gag and gently bathed Olivia's brow Sister Letitia said: "You took a fearful whipping, Olivia ... You did well."

Walpurga sat on the edge of the frame. She loved a girl with courage; it made the eventual seduction all the more enjoyable. The tunic stuck to her sweating thighs and breasts. Her nipples stood proudly erect. "You like my tits?" she asked, and before Olivia could utter a reply her hand was lifted to one of the damp breasts. The nipple was hard under her palm. "Squeeze," Walpurga urged.

Olivia obeyed; she had learnt that to do otherwise would be folly. Until she could find a way to escape she would remain dumbly obedient. Her fingers closed around the muscled globe, squeezing its firmness. Walpurga stared down at her without any show of emotion, although secretly she savoured the timid fumblings.

"She must go to the infirmary," Sister Letitia said, lifting the hand away.

"I shall take her there," Walpurga smiled evilly.

"And no doubt pass by your cell on the way."

Olivia gulped. Had she not suffered enough for one day without having to share the bed of this dark demon?

"Not at all," smiled Walpurga with incredible charm. "By Saint Dulcinea, I promise she shall be safely delivered."

"No," said Sister Letitia firmly. "If you must slake your voracious appetite, take Sister Alysoun or Sister Judith."

"I've had them already," she said dully and without enthusiasm.

Olivia wondered if there was anyone in the convent she hadn't had. It would take a great deal of resisting to escape her powerful clutches.

"So you might have done, but orders are orders. Do you think I intend to disobey the Novitiate Mistress, or the Abbess?"

Walpurga knew not to argue further - her time would come. She licked her lips as Sister Alysoun and Sister Judith carefully draped a light and airy smock over Olivia's punished body and helped her towards the door.

CHAPTER NINE

The Abbess sat in her window having her hair combed by the Novitiate Mistress. Olivia was being escorted across the courtyard below them just as a waggon rumbled in to deliver supplies. Both women watched her disappear out of sight through the infirmary door.

"Is she coming along well?" asked the Abbess.

"Her progress is satisfactory. So far she has submitted to both whip and rack."

"Willingly?"

"She is aware of her place within the order. But she needs watching."

"How so?"

"I caught her in the scriptorium, leafing through the sacred books."

The Abbess flashed an accusatory look at the Mistress. "You let her loose in there?"

The Mistress laid down the comb. "She saw nothing untoward. Even if she had, she would not have understood it. The little she saw of the books told her nothing too important."

The Abbess calmed a little. "Did you witness her on the rack?"

"I left that duty to Sister Letitia. I did hear the girl howl when she was whipped, but she is strong; she endured admirably."

The Abbess nodded with approval.

"She persists in her demands to see you however - she still insists upon leaving." The Mistress smiled. "But a spell in the infirmary has put paid to that for a while."

"I think it would be prudent if she did receive word from her friend," said the Abbess thoughtfully. "A telegram advising her to stay here for a while. Arrange for Sister Letitia to send one the next time she is on her rounds." She picked up a hand-mirror and checked her beauty with satisfaction. "Will the girl be ready for the ceremony?"

"I need a little more time to prepare her. The herbalist will take her through the next stage."

"When she has been prepared you will inform me, of course. No one else is to touch her."

The Mistress shuffled uneasily. "I'm afraid someone else already has, Reverend Mother."

The face of the Abbess clouded. "Who?"

"Walpurga."

"It's always Walpurga, isn't it. Days to prepare and moments to wreck."

"She is hot-blooded, she finds it difficult to control her urges. You know what gypsies are like; wild and tempestuous."

The Abbess was not appeased. "She can be as wild as she likes, but not with the new girl. I won't have her initiated between her thighs by anyone except me. I think Walpurga's urges need cooling. Have her put on the wheel, and then give her to those men."

"Men? Which men?"

"The ones unloading that waggon. I counted at least four of them. They'll keep her out of mischief for a while."

The Mistress bowed, smiled wickedly, and backed towards the door. "I'll see to it at once."

The Abbess called her back. "Then go to the woodworker and tell her to carve me the most beautiful specimen she has ever created - a perfect replica."

"At once, Reverend Mother." And she was gone with a swish of her habit.

The Abbess waited until the footsteps faded and the door at the end of the corridor closed. She then rose and slipped her gown from her shoulders. It rustled to the floor. She moved gracefully to her tall mirror. She studied her own voluptuous reflection, and a faint smile lifted the corners of her full lips. Her sparkling amber eyes drifted down to her firm breasts, which she cupped and flicked the stiffening nipples with her thumbs. A soft moan escaped her slightly parted lips and her long lashes fluttered. The Abbess was careful with her diet, as her flat stomach and lean thighs proved. She turned and looked over her shoulder to enjoy the view of her taut buttocks; they could have belonged to a girl of nineteen or twenty. She patted them, and then applied a short sharp slap. The flesh barely wobbled, and the sight of a pink handprint rising on the pale skin pleased her. The thought of administering similar treatment, and more, to the equally adorable Olivia thrilled her to the quick. No one else would be permitted to touch the girl ... not yet, at least.

A commotion of swearing and shouting coming from the courtyard below jolted her from her sweet reverie - Walpurga!

"Get your filthy hands off me!" Walpurga shrieked, hurling one of her fellow nuns to the ground.

"'Tis the wish of the Abbess that you be put on the wheel - so you may as well stop struggling!"

Walpurga's fist swung in a scything arc and cracked her other assailant on the jaw. A dozen more nuns came pouring from the refectory and joined in the melee. It took a good quarter-hour before Walpurga was finally overcome. By then her habit was in shreds and hung in tatters from her shoulders. As she stood panting the remains of the cloth were ripped from her back. Her dark body glistened with sweat. The delivery men stopped unloading the waggon and gawped like stunned sheep. It wasn't every day they saw one of the nuns naked in broad daylight.

"Take her to the wheel!" the Novitiate Mistress shouted, loud enough for the Abbess to hear.

Walpurga had made quite a few enemies in the convent with constant demands for her particular brand of sex. It was one of the rules that whoever was the recipient had to comply, and most of the nuns were heartily fed up with her and had at least one score to settle.

The men on the waggon watched in amazement as the gaggle of nuns dragged her to the wheel at the foot of the bell tower. She was still struggling, and managed to floor three of them before they were able to get her to the place of punishment.

The spoked wheel was perhaps eight feet in diameter. It was attached to a frame by the hub, with a handle on the rear side for turning. The rim was about six inches clear of the ground so it could revolve without hindrance. Walpurga stood facing it, her shoulders heaving.

"Step up," ordered the Mistress firmly. There was no need to shout now; the Abbess was watching from her window.

Walpurga, also aware that the Abbess was monitoring her behaviour, stepped humbly up onto the box which had been positioned by the wheel. She knew what to do. There was little point in further resistance.

"Thank you," one of the nuns said politely as Walpurga stretched out her arms.

Each wrist was tied to the rim by the attendant nuns. Her feet were not so easily roped. Grabbing an ankle apiece they forced open her powerful legs, leaving her temporarily suspended. For a few moments her arms took the weight while the nuns fumbled with the ropes, giving ample time for her body to take in the pain.

"Get on with it, you bitches!" she cursed.

But they delayed even more, arguing whether the ropes were suitable and of the right length. Then after much debate they secured her ankles to the rim, stretching her legs as wide as possible. Walpurga was now an alluring dark star of outstretched limbs.

One by one the speechless delivery men jumped down from their cart and joined the throng at the base of the tower.

"Who shall flog the miscreant?" asked the Mistress loud enough for all to hear.

Two nuns stepped forward simultaneously. The others were wary of Walpurga's vengeance.

"Fetch another stick," said the Mistress. "You may both administer the stripes. One above and one below. Decide for yourselves."

The nuns conferred and a decision was duly reached. "How many shall we give her, Mistress?" one of them asked.

"Twenty - evenly divided between the two of you."

Walpurga shuddered on the wheel. She would have shuddered a great deal more if she had but known the real intentions of the Abbess; young and beautiful females were more to her liking than the burly delivery men who were watching events with great interest. As yet they too were quite unaware of the pleasure that awaited them.

The Abbess seated herself in the window and peeled herself an apple. This promised to be an interesting distraction.

The Mistress nodded and the first lash whistled into

Walpurga's bottom. Her body tensed against the spokes. A harsh grunt broke the silence which had settled over the courtyard. The next stroke struck across her shoulders and encouraged another grunt. Walpurga was strong and could take the punishment, but the venting of anger and pain suddenly came as a flood of obscenities combined with a sensual writhing of hips.

The delivery men could not tear their eyes from the unexpected spectacle. "Those thighs," one of them nudged his mate, "did you ever see such a pair?" The men pushed forward, peering over the heads of the assembled nuns.

"What has she done to deserve such a thrashing?" one of them whispered.

A nun shrugged. "She is too free with herself. A more brazen bitch never roamed this convent."

"She is willing, then?"

"Willing?" the nun snorted derisively. "Aye, Walpurga is certainly willing." She smiled grimly. "The wheel will quash her appetite for a while though."

The wheel was actually beginning to turn slowly. Behind it two nuns were cranking the handle. The ropes binding Walpurga's wrist and ankle began to strain, whilst those which had been relieved of her weight went slack.

"You bastards!" Walpurga raged.

"All the way around with her!" encouraged one of the gathered audience.

"Yeah," agreed another. "She deserves it!"

As the wheel creaked slowly round the sticks continued to beat. Her bottom and lower back were criss-crossed with burning stripes.

"The purpose of the wheel," a nun explained in hushed tones to one of the delivery men beside her, "is that as it turns the punishment will strike every part of her body, except the front of course."

"I wonder the wench doesn't faint away," he said quite sincerely.

"Walpurga will last the full turn," the nun said with conviction.

By the time the wheel completed its cycle most of the assembled nuns and the delivery men secretly harboured some sympathy for the punished Walpurga.

"Take her down," the Mistress ordered.

The ropes were untied and Walpurga, shrugging away any offers of assistance, staggered away from the wheel. She turned and stood proudly before them all, clearly suffering but bravely doing her utmost to ignore the pain. She ran her fingers defiantly through her hair and tossed it back from her sweating face. "Am I free to go - Mistress?" she hissed.

The Mistress ignored her, and turning to the delivery men she said: "She is yours to do with as you please. Treat her as roughly as you like, but please leave her standing and capable of performing her daily chores on the morrow."

"I'll kill them first!" Walpurga spat.

The delivery men grinned and nudged each other; they liked a girl with spirit.

"You have until sunset," the Mistress concluded.

From her window high above the courtyard the Abbess saw the Mistress clap her hands and the gathered nuns slowly dispersing to their various places of duty. Once they had all departed the delivery men began to slowly stalk Walpurga. She hissed like a wild cat and slashed out with her nails and feet. One of the men made a sudden move to her right, and as she was distracted the other three overpowered her. Despite the flogging there was still plenty of fight left, but the men were gradually able to draw her nearer their waggon. The Abbess watched for a while longer, and then turned away and poured herself a tall glass of wine.

At sunset Walpurga picked her exhausted self up from the ground and watched the waggon rumble out through the gate.

"Enjoy your money!" shouted one of the delivery men as the gate slowly closed again. "You've earned it!"

She stooped and picked up the coin. Half a crown! She rubbed it between her fingers, and they turned a dull grey colour.

"You bastards!" echoed around the hushed walls of the convent. The coin bounced off the cobbled yard and rolled down a drain. Somewhere in the sewers lay a buckled lump of useless lead.

CHAPTER TEN

A driving rain swept across the convent courtyard as the Abbess made her way to the herbalist. The herbarium was situated in a corner of a smaller courtyard behind the former state apartments, so that the smoke and fumes from her fires wouldn't carry into the rest of the buildings. It was not a place the Abbess liked visiting. She wrinkled her nose in disgust as she forced open the door.

The herbalist was bent over her bench chopping a sheaf of leaves, humming to herself. All around the room were shelves lined with jars and bottles of varying shapes and sizes. Dead animals hung from hooks, waiting to be dissected. A fire blazed in the hearth sending clouds of smoke up the chimney. Because of the heat and poor ventilation, the herbalist nearly always worked in only her shift. She moved in the smoky atmosphere like a phantom. So engrossed was she in her work she didn't even notice the entrance of her Abbess.

"Sister Lupa," said the Abbess as she removed her wet cloak and shook it.

The herbalist jumped. She dropped the jar she was holding onto the bench and her stool clattered to the floor as she stood, wiping the grimy sweat from her brow. "Ah, Abbess," she smiled with a little annoyance at the abrupt interruption, and stooped to pick up the stool. "I've almost finished."

The Abbess looked past her at a small iron cauldron hanging over the fire. A thick yellow steam billowed from it. The smell was sickly-sweet, and very heady.

"Will it work?" she asked.

"Abbess, have you ever known one of my potions not to work?"

The Abbess held a handkerchief to her nose. Already she felt faint. "What is in this mind-muddling odour?" she complained.

"Mandrake, poppy, foxglove, and a pinch of belladonna," Sister Lupa announced proudly. "Taken in a goblet of red wine, and our little patient will be none the wiser."

The Abbess wrinkled her nose - she seriously doubted that. "Does she trust you?"

"Implicitly. I've been tending to her day and night. She has fully recovered from the rack."

"And what happens after she's drunk your evil smelling potion?"

"Nothing for a while. She'll fall into a deep sleep, and when she wakes she'll do exactly as you wish, although I doubt that she'll recognize you. But she will be aware of what's happening to her - I can assure you of that."

"She must be responsive. There'll be no pleasure in

seducing her otherwise."

"She will be."

"And capable of the tiniest little resistance - just to add to my fun?"

Sister Lupa smiled knowingly. "She'll be all that you want her to be; whatever you choose."

The Abbess tingled at the prospect. "Excellent! When will you administer it to her?"

Sister Lupa took up a large wooden spoon and stirred the cauldron. The yellow steam turned a dirty brown and the brew bubbled and spat like volcanic lava.

"Within the hour."

"And she will be ready for me, when?"

"I should say midnight, or thereabouts."

The anticipation left the Abbess breathless, not to mention the cloying heat of the herbarium. She swung her cloak back around her shoulders and opened the door. The cold rain hit her face and the cool fresh air instantly made her feel better. "I shall go now to my quarters ..." she looked back to Sister Lupa with a glint in her amber eyes, "... and make myself ready."

"Midnight," Sister Lupa confirmed. "She'll be ready for you by midnight. Enjoy."

Left in peace, she distilled a little of the contents of the cauldron into a jug. When it was cool she added a bottle of the convent's own red wine. She stirred the blend thoroughly, and then went to her room behind the herbarium to wash and change into a freshly laundered habit, as all good nurses should.

CHAPTER ELEVEN

Olivia lay in bed in the infirmary. She thought it a little strange there were no other sick nuns with her, but was pleased there weren't. The peace and quiet was just what she needed.

The Mistress had brought her a telegram. It was from Flora, telling her to stay where she was for a while longer until she could arrange to have her collected. There was no indication of how long that might be. Olivia was deflated, to say the least, but she already had another idea forming. Her only chance of getting away now was in one of those delivery waggons, and then she would have to beg her way to Ottery, or back to London. This whole venture had been a disaster, and London now seemed like a safe haven by comparison. There must be some kind people out there who would help a young lady in trouble - surely!

The handsome nun who had helped bring her to the convent came into the dormitory, carrying a tray with bread and a jug of wine. For some reason Olivia felt she could trust her.

"Here we are," said Sister Lupa, setting down the tray. "Bread fresh from the oven and wine from our very own cellars."

"Oh," said Olivia weakly, "I'm not sure I should drink alcohol."

"Nonsense - it'll do you good." Sister Lupa broke the

loaf and poured a generous goblet of rich wine. It ran blood-red from the jug in the glow of the setting sun which peeped through the heavy rain-clouds that rumbled past. She told Olivia to drink every last drop, and to make haste because she was due at the chapel for evening worship and she wouldn't leave until she was sure her patient had taken all her meal. Olivia ate and drank with gusto, and was surprised just how hungry and thirsty she was once she started. Quickly the bread and wine were devoured. With a smile of satisfaction which Olivia mistook for kindness Sister Lupa settled her patient for the night and left.

Olivia snuggled down, feeling warm and comfortable. The wine made her feel good. She rolled onto her side and nestled under the crisp warm sheets. From the direction of the bell tower came a dolorous tolling. Olivia counted the strikes and slowly drifted into a heavy slumber.

She had no idea what time it was when she awoke. She listened to the unfamiliar hooting of owls and some animal or other scurrying across the window-ledge outside and scraping the glass as it tried to get in. She rolled onto her back and tucked the sheet tightly beneath her chin. With bleary eyes she stared at the vaulted ribs of the ceiling. In the dim candlelight they wavered to and fro, went out of focus, and then cleared again. Olivia blinked rapidly, trying to clear her fuzzy head, and then groaned as gradually the whole ceiling began to spin, gaining speed, faster and faster. The plain stone tiles seemed dotted with tiny specks of light, twinkling like stars - and in the middle a shape gradually formed … a naked woman swooping from the night sky! Olivia gave a cry of fright and tried to summon Sister Lupa with the small bell which had been left on the bedside unit for that very purpose, but no matter how hard she tried she couldn't raise her hand to it. Her body had turned to jelly, the limbs limp and useless. She seemed to be floating upwards now, or was the vision still coming down to meet her.

"Help me..." Olivia wailed.

The beautiful vision was almost on top of her. Olivia could feel her sweet breath wafting against her cheek. It was just a bad dream; the wine disagreeing with her. It had to be.

But the vision was breathtakingly real. Despite her fear Olivia couldn't tear her eyes from it. It - she, climbed onto the bed and straddled Olivia's thighs, her own legs apart, the smile on her face devastatingly beautiful. Olivia closed her eyes, hoping the vision would be gone when she looked again, but now all she could see was the overhead painting in the punishment room. She began to feel ill; the tighter she screwed her eyes the faster the stars span. She opened them again and the vision stared back at her with hypnotic amber eyes as wide as saucers. When the owl hooted again it was deafening, filling the whole dormitory and bouncing off the walls and ceiling.

Olivia began to shiver. The vision hovered inches above, her face blurring and somehow evaporating. With immense effort Olivia reached up and touched the tumbling hair and a soft warm cheek. It felt so real! She had to be real!

The vision took Olivia's hand and stroked it gently. She kissed each fingertip, and then slipped them one by one between her moistened lips. As the vision suckled a delicious calm emanated from her warm mouth and seeped into Olivia's whole body. Never had she felt so tranquil or so still ... or so wonderfully aroused. Her nipples tingled and stiffened, and she mumbled only a token resistance when the vision folded down the blanket and sheet, untied the drawstring of her cotton nightgown, laid it open, and bent to take one of the willing buds into her mouth. For what seemed an eternity the hardened teat was nipped by teasing teeth and rolled and flicked by an incredibly skilful tongue. The mouth gradually opened wider and more of Olivia's breast forced inside.

A hand rested softly on her thigh and stroked; a touch she felt, and yet did not feel. The fingers barely glanced on her responsive skin, but the grip was firm, squeezing and progressing steadily higher. Olivia started and held her breath when the hand closed around her sex, the fingers gliding into her wet portal. They penetrated without waiting for any form of permission - just as Olivia prayed they would. The vision seemed to know exactly what Olivia needed, before she even did herself.

"Please ..." whimpered Olivia. "Please don't torture me. I can't bear it. Please ..."

The vision lifted from Olivia's yearning breasts and gracefully slithered down her body. The blanket and sheet rustled and were gone, and then Olivia felt her nightgown being tugged up her thighs and under her bottom until it lay around her middle. "What is it you want?" the vision softly coaxed. "What is it you desire the most?"

"You." The admission was out into the tense atmosphere before Olivia had time to gather her befuddled thoughts.

"Me?" Hot breath tickled Olivia's twitching belly. "You desire me more than anything else in the world?"

Olivia sobbed. She could feel her juices anointing the persistent fingers and her thighs instinctively opened to allow easier access. If her words didn't give her away, her body surely would. "Yes, whatever - whoever you are, I need you to do as you wish with me."

"Of course you do," she heard, and then lips kissed her labia and a tongue found and flicked her clitoris. Olivia stiffened and arched her back; only her heels, arms, and shoulders touched the soft mattress. Her fingers clawed the bottom sheet. A hand cupped and squeezed her buttocks, and another stroked up her flat belly and ribcage to caress her panting breasts. She groaned with frustration as the generous mouth left her all too soon, but she knew there were more and even more exquisite delights to come.

Olivia's knees were eased wider apart and the vision knelt between them. Lips fluttered against her forehead and closed eyelids, and fingers coated with her own musk slipped into her mouth. A mass of auburn hair tumbled around her. Olivia gasped for air and the fingers were replaced by a persistent tongue which danced against her own. She locked her arms and legs around the vision, not wanting her to disappear. Something large and solid nudged into her groin. She groaned into the hot mouth locked against her own. Her mind returned to the scriptorium and the images she saw in the books. The figure which was neither man or woman span through her head.

"Who are you?" she pleaded, pulling away.

The vision looked down at her with an inscrutable smile and gave a gentle thrust of her loins. Olivia tensed. Her blurred eyes saw the inviting breasts hovering just above her. They swayed firmly to and fro, the erect nipples asking to be sucked. Another gentle urge and her labia sucked around the phallus.

"It's so hard," she sobbed.

"And it's all for you," the vision whispered, and sank a little deeper.

Through her delirium Olivia knew the invading object could not be real; knew it was not of flesh and blood. It was too solid; there was no warmth in its contours. Yet as Olivia adjusted herself around it, shuffling her bottom and snaking her hips, it felt real enough. The vision gave one last push of her loins and Olivia gasped and raised her face to the comforting warmth between the swinging breasts. She was fully penetrated.

Arms squeezed between the mattress and her shoulders and hugged her tight. The two women kissed, breast against breast, nipple against nipple. The bed began to spin again, carrying them up to the starry sky.

"I saw you painted on the ceiling," Olivia whispered. "How is it you're alive inside me?"

"I am not dead," she replied, "but come alive to lie with you. Feel me. Engulf my rod."

They rolled onto their sides, a confused tangle of limbs, hands and tongues, never still for a second. The temperature between them soared. Perspiration glowed on their faces and backs. Olivia's throat was parched.

"Now we are one," the vision whispered. "Joined together, never to part. Feel me inside you, Olivia. Embrace me."

Olivia's vagina hugged the shaft, the muscles moving against it, feeling their way to its bulbous head. It were as if she had a man riding her. The penis was solid enough, but the body that held her was different. There were no rippling muscles on the torso, the arms were not powerfully built, nor the chest flat. Only the rigid shaft was real. Now it was moving, a gentle thrusting of hips and loins, and always the skin so soft and feminine against her.

Suddenly Olivia shook uncontrollably. The writhing body in her arms was a foreign land of soft undulating hills and valleys, a forest of sweet smelling flowers, a pool of unknown depths. She was drowning in its waters, being sucked to the bottom.

The vision gripped Olivia's buttocks. Their groins pressed together. Olivia searched blindly for her seducer's sex. She found the hard base of the shaft sprouting from within. Could it be possible that both of them were penetrated by the same organ; bound together, riding the same beast, sharing the same glorious sensations? Olivia pushed her hips against those of her phantom lover, riding in unison, responding with a mirror image of every thrust and heave.

"You make love like an angel," the vision whispered. "Spread your wings and fly."

Olivia was flying. Her body was soaring to the stars revolving around her. "I can't get enough of you," she rasped desperately. "You feel so wonderful."

"Better than any mortal," whispered the vision.

"I - what do you - Ooh!" Olivia was silenced as the phallus filled her again.

"You make me work very hard to satisfy you." The gentle monotone was hypnotic. "Say not a word more, and let me take you to places you never dreamed possible."

Olivia closed her eyes and drifted on a white cloud of ecstasy. The poor bed creaked faster and faster beneath the powerful lunges. She grunted as their bellies slapped together again and again. She thought this bliss would never end. "Kiss me!" she heard from somewhere. "Kiss me, Olivia!"

Their lips mashed together and Olivia climaxed loudly into the open and sucking mouth of her lover. The orgasm drained her; she was totally spent. She slumped into the mattress and lay without moving, save for the heavy swell of her breasts. "I've come ..." she murmured drowsily.

The beautiful vision cupped Olivia's face. "You have so much to learn, my angel," she whispered huskily. "But I shall teach you, and given time you will understand everything."

The lovely face blurred.

"I'm so tired," moaned Olivia.

"Rest then. Sleep contented. You are one of us now."

Olivia swooned under more stroking and kissing. She was too drained to do otherwise. Her limbs refused to move and offer any embrace in return. She just lay still, breathing deeply. The gorgeous penis slipped from her. It rested a while on her stomach - wet and warm. Showers of tiny kisses sprinkled over her face and breasts, sending her towards restful sleep. She curled into a tight ball and muttered incoherently. She was at peace, but the images she had glimpsed in the books and seen in the chapel drifted through her dreams - sometimes lucid, and at other times a vague apparition. She saw naked women cavorting with devils. She saw angels fondly embracing. She heard the creaking of rollers and levers and the lashing of whips. She heard tormented wails and screams, and tried to close her mind to them all.

The bed creaked as the vision left her, and soft footsteps retreated into the candlelit gloom.

CHAPTER TWELVE

"It must have been the wine after all," Sister Lupa said, drawing back the crumpled sheets.

Olivia sat up and rubbed her throbbing temples. Her throat felt as if it had been rubbed with sandpaper.

"A dream," she murmured. "A terrible nightmare. The ceiling changed. I saw stars and a woman." She looked up at the vaulted roof. Nothing had changed; stone ribs and flaking paint. "She came down from the sky and made love to me, right here on this very bed." Her hand moved sheepishly between her legs. Her labia felt tender. Under her bottom the sheet was damp. She tried to recall more of her dream, but it only returned in fragments; not enough to give a clear account. But she did remember the inanimate organ that gave her so much pleasure.

"How could that be?" Sister Lupa asked. "You said it was a woman who came to you."

Then Olivia remembered. "The painted ceiling in the punishment room. It was her - I swear it."

"Gosh, you were dreaming. That painting is of the Abbess who was persecuted and driven here by the Holy Inquisition."

"Well?"

"My dear Olivia, do you not know your history? That was over four hundred years ago. Now be a good girl and drink up your milk."

Olivia was still not convinced. It had been more than a dream. It was so vivid she had seen starry skies above, had been made love to by a beautiful hermaphrodite, and she now sat in the evidence of her own passions. She shuddered as a terrible thought dawned on her.

"Sister Lupa, do you think I'm going mad?"

"Don't be so silly," she laughed dismissively. "You're much better now, and the Mistress has said you can get up today. I think she wants you to help the seamstress."

Olivia dressed slowly, thinking things over. She knew she had been tricked into coming here, Sister Letitia had said so. She thought of her plan to escape in one of the visiting waggons, but it might be ages before another delivery arrived, and by then it might be too late for her. She dared not think of what horrors might befall her in this godforsaken place.

She brushed her hair and then paced up and down the dormitory. An idea quickly came to mind, utterly foolish, but it might just work. Her heart thumped. All she needed was a scrap of paper and a pencil. She would write a note, saying who and where she was. She had seen the ravens flying around the convent and had noticed they were tame enough for the nuns to feed from the hand. If she could attach the note to one it might get carried to a town or something. It was ridiculous, but no matter how remote the possibility, she had to give it a try. There was nothing else left.

To her great relief Sister Lupa saw no objection in writing a note to Flora, telling her she was quite happy to stay there until things were sorted out. Fortunately she left Olivia alone after bringing the paper and pencil and Olivia, thinking fast, wrote one note to Flora and another to whoever might find it. Then she opened the window and spread crumbs all over the sill. She scattered a few more inside the dormitory and sat down to wait. It wasn't long before her messenger arrived, a remarkably docile creature, so stupid it went on picking at the crumbs while she tied her note to one of its legs. Then she chased it out of the window and watched it go flapping over the battlements, struggling to gain height with the weight of its fat belly pulling it earthward. Thank God no one she knew in London was here to witness this; a young lady living in the nineteenth century, trapped in a mediaeval convent and tying distress messages to the legs of a bird. She had to keep reminding herself, as she made her way to the seamstress, that she was not mad. It was her only practical hope. Anyone else would have done the same.

It was late afternoon when the Mistress found Olivia quietly sewing a torn habit.

"The Abbess wishes to speak with you, Miss Holland." Her eyes twinkled behind her glasses. "I think she's had a change of heart."

The habit fell from Olivia's hands. "She has? You mean, I'm free to go?"

"Let's just say you don't have to do that any more." And

she took Olivia's hand and led her to the Abbess.

At last she had an audience with the high priestess of this madhouse. She laughed at the thought of how she had tied a piece of paper to the raven. With luck no one would find it now she was going to be released. What a silly idea that had been. It must be Flora, come to get her out. She was still smiling when the Mistress opened a door and ushered her inside.

Olivia seated herself on a stool before a large desk as requested. The Abbess was sitting behind the desk, and as Olivia looked up her heart sank and her complexion drained. Her hands shook. Should she tell the Abbess about her dream and how closely the Abbess resembled the woman who had plundered her? No, that would be unwise. No need to complicate things now that she was about to be rid of the place.

"What is the matter?" the Abbess asked, smiling casually.

"Oh, nothing," Olivia managed. "I'm just tired."

"You had a bad night? Well, we all get those from time to time. And sometimes it makes us become irrational, doing things we wouldn't ordinarily do, behaving in ways we wouldn't ordinarily behave."

Olivia's heart sank further. "I'm sure I don't know what you mean."

"I think you do," the Abbess said ominously. "I was unaware that your husband is a barrister at Lincolns Inn."

Olivia crossed her legs and started fidgeting with her sleeve. Her nipples tingled and pushed at the cotton. Her foot tapped nervously on the floor. Her eyes lowered to avoid the piercing amber stare. How on earth could the Abbess know about Rupert? Had she confided in anybody since arriving here? No … It could only be …

At that moment there was a ferocious beating of wings and Olivia looked up again.

"Miss Holland, I'd like you to meet Judas," the Abbess smiled as the odious creature settled on her desk, "my pet raven. He's so handsome - don't you think?"

Words hid from Olivia, and despite opening her mouth none were forthcoming.

"And *so* loyal to me."

"Look ... your grace," Olivia found the words and stammered, still unfamiliar with the correct form of address. "I said I had a bad dream, and you said yourself that a lack of good sleep makes us become -"

"So irrational that we tie a note to the leg of a bird in the hope that a knight in shining armour will come to the rescue?" The Abbess was cruelly mocking poor Olivia. "My dear child - that sort of happy ending only occurs in fairy tales. I suppose you were going to live happily ever after?"

Tears blurred Olivia's vision. She sniffed and wiped her eyes with her sleeve. Not only had her hopes of escaping been totally quashed, but she also felt like a foolish infant.

"I'm afraid the silly note never had a chance of reaching your hero-knight. It arrived on my desk only minutes after you'd written it." She turned to the wretched creature and stroked it under the beak. "He probably assumed it was addressed to me - didn't you, Judas."

Olivia could have killed it there and then. "I didn't know it was a friend of yours," she said bitterly.

"Probably the most reliable I have," she smiled, leaning forward until her breasts rested on the desktop. She clasped her hands together as if in prayer and closed her eyes. Her habit was cut low, and Olivia surreptitiously glanced at the ample flesh bulging and threatening to burst free.

"It's all due to those couple of days in the infirmary," the Abbess said at length. "Lazing on your back with nothing more to do than touch yourself sinfully."

"I didn't!" Olivia pleaded her innocence. "I did no such thing!"

"That is not what Sister Lupa tells me. Apparently the evidence of your guilt clearly marked your sheets this morning."

Olivia blushed profusely. She could not deny the sheets. "But, I -"

"A passionate young lady such as yourself needs something to occupy her mind, and her body."

This sounded sinister.

"You will therefore wait at the tables in the refectory this supper."

Olivia sighed quietly; she was expecting a severe punishment, but waiting on tables didn't sound too bad.

"Now get out."

CHAPTER THIRTEEN

"Take off your habit and come along with me," said the Mistress.

"Take off my habit?"

"You have to be in the refectory at once. Supper is early this evening."

"But not naked, surely?"

"Yes naked," said the Mistress, reaching for the fastening of Olivia's clothing. "You are serving the Sisters to learn obedience and humility. And being naked will teach you just that. So please undress."

Olivia stepped back - she didn't want to be touched by the woman any more - and drew the habit over her head. They left the cell and went to the kitchens, where she was given a silver salver. Coiled upon it was a long leather belt. She followed behind the Mistress, holding the plate before her at breast level.

When the couple entered the refectory the nuns weren't sitting at the benches as Olivia expected, but were standing in two long lines, facing each other to form a human corridor. At the far end on a raised dais the Abbess sat elegantly. Olivia was positioned by the Mistress at the beginning of the two rows. The first nun to her right lifted the belt from the salver and allowed it to uncoil. It was long and almost swept to the floor.

"You will walk one step at a time between the Sisters," the Mistress announced ceremonially. "And as you do so, the belt will be passed from one to the other all the way down the line. You will look straight ahead at all times and carry the salver to the Abbess. Then you will await her pleasure."

This was disgraceful, but Olivia knew better than to complain. She took one faltering step, proudly holding her head high and not looking at the Abbess but at the fresco above and behind her. If she could concentrate on that she might make it. It seemed the whole convent had assembled between the benches. She wondered where they had all come from, for the sole purpose of humiliating her, beating her one at a time. They would stare at her nakedness while they whipped her. She was the lowest of the whole rotten heap, a plaything, there to be used and abused by anyone at all. She knew now that the only way out had to be in one of those waggons. She grit her teeth and brought her feet together - waiting.

The belt whistled and landed on her bottom with a loud crack. Her body quivered from the blow and she took another painful step. The belt was passed behind her to the nun on the opposite side. She wrapped it around her hand

and it slashed diagonally from right shoulder to left hip. Olivia reeled from the scorching pain. Her back arched and the edge of the salver pressed into her nipples. The belt passed behind her back again in readiness for a fresh strike. Another step. Eyes fixed to the fresco, and again the swish and searing pain.

The Abbess seemed a longer way away and the nuns more numerous every time she stole a glance at their leering faces.

The lash that whistled into her thighs seemed to burn right to the bone. She stood still, holding back a sob. Already her bottom and back were ablaze, yet she had not even taken five miserable paces. They were each beating her harder than the last. Perhaps there was a reward for the one who finally brought her to her knees, a sobbing wreck begging for mercy. She would never reach the Abbess if it continued like this.

She fixed her eyes on the fresco; another painted wheel with naked figures in it. The centre-piece was a woman rising from a blazing furnace, arms raised to the sky, while men and women copulated all around her. Olivia grit her teeth and awaited the next blow.

At every lash that whipped into her thighs she managed one step closer the dais. Failure to complete the course was not a consideration. She would get through this disgraceful treatment. Afterwards, somehow, she would make her escape, and when she returned it would be with a vengeance. She would see every last one of these so called nuns imprisoned - see if she didn't.

Olivia had lost count of the number of strokes suffered by the time she staggered to the end of the line and humbly handed the salver to the waiting Abbess.

"Am I punished enough?" she whimpered.

"Enough for now," the Abbess replied. "You may now

fulfill your punishment by waiting at the tables."

Olivia couldn't decide which was the most humiliating; being flogged naked by the whole convent or having to fetch and carry for them. She went to the kitchen and brought back trays laden with bowls of soup. She hadn't laid the first table when she realized why she had been told to do that; the nuns patted her bottom as they might a child on its head for being good. Others felt between her legs. Neither did they spare her breasts. Her nipples were pinched sore by the time she'd fetched the last of the trays.

The nuns bolted down their food amid a cacophony of excited chatter, while Olivia ate alone in a corner, resting her poor bottom on a silk cushion which had been considerately provided. As she ate she studied the fresco. The woman rising from the flames was similar to the one in the punishment chamber and the one she had dreamed in her arms. But in this painting the colours were vibrant, fresh and newly painted. Olivia nearly choked when she recognized the face of the Abbess. The similarity was striking, and yet they were apparently separated by more than four centuries! Around this central character and the copulating couples were more strange codes and symbols. Every facet of life in the convent seemed governed by ritual and law that everyone dumbly obeyed without question. Suddenly it occurred to Olivia that in a short space of time she had already witnessed floggings in the chapel, had heard that Walpurga had been put on the wheel and then handed over to four tradesmen, and yet no one appeared to actually want or even attempt an escape. It didn't seem natural that amongst a body of women continually subjected to suffering at the slightest pretext, not one showed the slightest desire to flee. Indeed it seemed the complete opposite. They were content behind the fortified walls, having little communication with the outside world, wrapped up in their bizarre books and paintings.

A strange feeling crept through Olivia. Perhaps all this behaviour was quite normal and it was she who was not. Were they in some way being truthful with themselves? Had they the honesty to come to terms with their own hidden desires?

"Miss Holland."

A large nun interrupted Olivia's thoughts.

"You're needed over here - and bring your cushion."

Olivia went to where the nun sat and reached for some of the dirty dishes, noticing that a number had already been cleared and a space left on the table.

"Leave those plates and climb up here," said the large nun, patting the wooden surface before her with a broad grin on her round face.

Olivia was beyond complaining. She climbed onto the bench and then rolled onto the cushion which had been positioned for her.

"What do you want from me now?" she groaned wearily.

The nuns giggled like spoilt schoolgirls. "We want to see you pleasure yourself," said one.

Olivia closed her eyes in acceptance. "If I must," she whispered.

Hands initiated the proceedings by pulling her ankles apart and raising her knees. Without hesitation, but with contempt for her audience, she slipped her fingers between her thighs. She would attempt to close her mind to everything around her; the prying eyes, the lustful stares, the crowding faces. If they wanted to see her masturbate to orgasm, then so be it.

But that was easier thought than done, for the nuns closed in, stalking around her like predatory she-wolves. One took her head and held it rigid. Others pinched and squeezed her breasts. Fingers tweaked her nipples. Her widespread ankles were lifted and came to rest on the shoulders of those whose hands possessed and stroked her thighs.

Olivia concentrated between her legs, sliding her fingers in and out. Tongues lapped at her eyelids and ears, and fingers slipped into her gasping mouth. Teeth nipped her arms and belly. Wet lips kissed her toes. Olivia couldn't breath. They swamped her. They were gorging themselves as though she was the main course to their banquet. Were they all deranged?! She wanted to flee, but knew it was hopeless. She had not the strength to deny the frantic hands and mouths that pinned her to the table. Suddenly she wanted to see the perpetrators. She opened her eyes to the sea of ecstatic bobbing faces, and was immediately kissed full on the mouth. The wetted fingers she had been sucking were thrust in alongside her own, moving in unison and probing deep.

The nuns were shrieking and pinching and prodding like frenzied warriors gloating over their captive prize. Habits were hastily shed. Bodies intertwined and writhed between welcoming outstretched thighs.

Through lowered lashes Olivia saw the round-faced nun drooling down at her, and heard her pant through the mayhem: "Come on then dearie, let me help you," and with that Olivia felt strong fingers cover her own and drive them back and forth across her aching bud. Olivia's back arched. She squealed. The nun held her gaze with that same broad grin, and Olivia erupted beneath her.

Gradually the nuns dispersed.

"You can find your own way back to your cell," said the Mistress, throwing a habit onto the table beside her. "Sister Lupa will attend to you in the morning."

Olivia knew not how long she lay on the table, half asleep, yet unable to find peace. Even though she was alone the place seemed full of sound; whispers that came from nowhere, furtive rustlings in the shadows, and footsteps that seemed both near and far. As the fires died in the hearths cold set in and Olivia rose and stiffly slipped into the habit. Amongst the uncleared dishes she found a jug with a little water in the bottom. She gratefully swallowed the few drops and then unhappily tossed the jug to the flags. It shattered into a hundred pieces.

Rubbing life back into her aching limbs Olivia made her way along the passage and stepped out into the dark cold courtyard.

"Olivia!"

A hand clawed her shoulder. She spun around and prepared to strike. "You ..?!"

CHAPTER FOURTEEN

Walpurga clamped her hand over Olivia's mouth and dragged her into the shadows. A lamp lit in one of the cells was trimmed and the shutters closed after it. Walpurga let out her breath in a long, relieved sigh. "Lupa," she whispered. "She's waiting for her lover."

"What are you doing here?" Olivia whispered in surprise as the powerful fingers released her jaw, her heart still pounding from the shock.

"If you want to escape this place, come with me."

Walpurga ghosted silently across the courtyard, with Olivia stumbling behind, trying to keep up. They ducked into a ruined tower and regained their breath. Olivia listened to the sound of water running from somewhere below.

"The stream," Walpurga answered her inquisitive look.

"That's where all the slops are emptied. We'll have to go through the water gate, it's our only hope."

Olivia didn't have time to think or ask why Walpurga was helping her. She just followed blindly, half expecting the whole scenario to be another trick. The two women crawled on their hands and knees along the bottom of the curtain-wall to a small culvert. The sound of the water was louder and nearer now. A slime-covered iron grill across a low arch hung open.

"That's a bit of luck!" panted Walpurga.

"What is?" asked Olivia, trying to keep up with this sudden and unexpected turn of events.

"The grill - it should be closed. I thought we'd have a bit of a problem there!"

Olivia didn't need telling twice to crawl under the arch, and then she balanced precariously along the narrow ledge just above the swirling freezing water. Walpurga was close behind. Olivia shrieked and nearly lost her grip as a rat darted from a crack in the crumbling brickwork and plunged into the water so close by she could have touched it. Thankfully they were soon both out of that stinking place and on the other side of the great walls, heaving great lungfuls of chilled fresh air.

"I …" Olivia panted with difficulty. "I'm very grateful to you … But why are you helping me?"

"I was put on the wheel because of you … and then given to those bastard men!" Walpurga hissed with an intensity that frightened Olivia. "This is my way of paying back the Abbess."

"By … helping me escape? But I don't understand."

Walpurga sniggered, her breathing calming somewhat. "Imagine her face when she finds the pair of us gone. There'll be all hell to pay for the others."

"But why will she be so angry?"

"Why? Because she hates me, and would take great pleasure in punishing me further. And because she adores you, and wants you for her own."

Olivia stared into the night as Walpurga's words sank in, and then she scurried after her up the slippery bank and into the woods.

"What on earth do you - ?"

"Shhh!" Walpurga silenced her with a sharp but harmless slap to the face. "Do you want to wake the whole convent?"

Olivia rubbed her tingling cheek, feeling rather stupid. "I'm sorry," she apologized meekly.

Her habit had ripped on the undergrowth and brambles. Walpurga gripped it and tore the long skirts away so that it reached to just below her knees. She modified her own in a similar fashion, and with their increased mobility they made their way along a well-trodden path winding through the moonlit trees. At least Walpurga seemed to know where she was going.

"Only another mile or two," she eventually said over her shoulder. "Then we can rest awhile. Tomorrow morning we shall ride the rest of the way."

"I have to get to Ottery," Olivia said, hoping they were heading in that direction.

Walpurga said nothing, but walked all the faster. Her long legs carried her easily over streams and branches. Olivia knew her own strength was failing. After a little longer Walpurga thankfully called a halt to their progress.

"You're struggling," she said, eyeing the evidence of Olivia's pained expression and heaving breasts.

"A little … yes."

She looked around a little nervously. "We'll sleep here, then." There was a hint of irritation in her voice. Olivia knew she would have liked to put quite a lot more distance behind them; a few lights could still be seen from the dreadful convent.

"Tell me about the wheel," Olivia said when they eventually settled beneath a thick bush and a blanket of fallen leaves.

Walpurga wrapped her powerful arms around Olivia's shoulders and drew her close until her head rested between her breasts. Olivia gingerly cuddled her rescuer, and felt more at peace than she had for quite some time.

"The wheel? There's not really very much to tell. It's just a cartwheel on a drum that turns when you're tied to it and flogged."

Olivia shuddered.

"You turn full circle, upside down and then upright, and you're whipped to the blood in the meantime."

"You suffered that because of me?"

Walpurga lifted Olivia's chin and kissed her with surprising delicacy. "Don't think I went through that hell for nothing. You owe me."

"Oh. Well, what do you want from me?" As if Olivia didn't know.

"You'll find out soon enough. Now go to sleep - we have a long way to go in the morning."

The night passed quickly in slumber, made more deep in the safety of each others arms. Olivia nuzzled close, and Walpurga's habit inched open until the sleeping girl's sweet breath tickled over her nipple. Walpurga awoke first in the grey dawn, and smiled to herself. Olivia's soft lips were slightly apart as she slept so innocently, and Walpurga craftily lifted her nipple into her waiting mouth. Olivia suckled instinctively, and Walpurga crushed her all the tighter. She tingled with pleasure and moved her hand into Olivia's habit and over her warm bottom, sliding it into the cleft and softly kneading the delicious cheeks.

Olivia stirred and looked up with clear eyes. "Would

you like me to please you?" she whispered, feeling somewhat indebted to her companion.

"Yes - but not now, we have no time. And why do you ask? Was it not me who tortured you on the rack?"

"You were only doing your duty."

"Not strictly true. I enjoyed it, seeing your body stretched out like that. I couldn't resist touching you. That's why the Abbess had me flogged. I was too forward. I should have waited my turn. But then Flora would have had you first."

Olivia stiffened. "Who - ?!"

Walpurga stared in disbelief as swarthy hands thrust through their protective foliage, seized Olivia by the throat, and yanked her to her feet. The stunned victim was spun round like a doll. Another hand gripped the habit and ripped it clean off with a single tug. Then it pushed her on the chest and sent her tumbling over her companion. They were on them in seconds, stripping Walpurga and binding them both with rope, their hands tied at their fronts.

"Bring 'em over 'ere!" hollered a gruff male voice.

The speechless and fearful pair were dragged and hauled through the trees to a nearby clearing, where waited a ramshackle cart. The ropes were secured to iron rings on the vehicles tailgate. The ambushers surrounded them; a group of evil-looking tinkers with bulging eyes that surveyed every naked inch of their prey.

Walpurga and Olivia inched away until their backs nudged against the cart and they could go no further.

"'Ow comes you're out 'ere in the woods all by yourselves then?" one asked stepping forward, presumably the leader.

"We're nuns," Olivia said quickly, hoping that might offer a reprieve. "You have no right to be treating us like this."

Walpurga groaned and lifted her eyes to the trees.

"Nuns? Whores more like. I never seed nuns wiv bare legs an' tits out in these woods before." He looked around his comrades with a toothless grin. "'Ave you boys?"

There was a general murmuring and shaking of heads.

The leader stepped close and slapped Walpurga's bottom. "A nice arse for a nun," he complimented. Then he put an arm around her waist and mauled her breasts. Olivia leapt forward in defence of her new friend but another tinker, with surprising agility, grabbed her arms painfully and pushed her back to back against Walpurga.

The men closed in. Their rancid breath combined with Olivia's fear to make her feel sick. She lowered her gaze to the overgrown ground. Tobacco stained fingers lifted her chin and without allowing her time to respond wet lips slobbered over hers. She tried to squirm away but more hands held her tight and roamed over her breasts and flanks and thighs. Stout fingers worked into her groin and she struggled to dislodge them. "I likes a lass what's got a bit o' fight in 'er!" her assailant wheezed in her face.

"Come on lads!" the leader suddenly stepped away and cuffed a few of his own team firmly around the head. "We got some earnin's t'collect!"

The foul group scurried up onto the cart, but not without cursing and promising the two captives more of the same if the chance arose.

With a click of his gums and a flick of a whip the leader encouraged the flea-bitten and overworked mule to pull them all to the nearest track. The cart lurched and creaked, and Olivia and Walpurga could do nothing but trudge along behind.

Eventually the motley collection turned onto a rutted and puddled track. Although disorientated, both captives knew in which direction they were headed.

The three men slouched on the back of the cart leered and winked at their cargo, rubbing their clearly standing erections through their filthy breeches. Olivia shuddered with disgust, and then noticed from the corner of her eye Walpurga smiling at them and licking her lips.

"What are you doing?" she whispered in astonishment from the side of her mouth.

"You know where they intend taking us, don't you?" Walpurga returned between directing extravagantly sexy kisses and pouts at the men.

"Yes, but -"

"Then do as I do. It's our only chance."

"I won't. I -"

"Boys," Walpurga cooed sexily at the men, ignoring Olivia's protests. "We're ever so thirsty back here."

"Walpurga!" Olivia hissed under her breath. "Don't you dare!"

"If you'd stop awhile and let us drink something, we'd be *ever so* grateful."

The rough crew couldn't hide their boyish excitement, and there ensued a mumbled conference with the leader who drove the cart with his back to them all. The debate was only interrupted by the occasional glance he threw over his shoulder at the two lovely females. He knew to deprive his men of such beauties could well lead to mutiny, and besides, his own erection had grown to considerably uncomfortable proportions - and he fancied doing some pretty obscene things to the innocent looking one with the gorgeous tits. He sent a ball of spittle arching into the undergrowth and then pulled the cart off the track to where it would be unseen from any other vehicle that might happen to pass by.

"Come on then boys," he said, jumping down from his seat. "Let's 'ave us some fun."

"Keep them happy, Olivia," Walpurga whispered secretly as the four loomed upon them. "It's our only chance of escape."

"I hope you're right Walpur - !" was all Olivia could manage before a short fat member of the gang grabbed her and the leader shoved a rusty knife before her eyes. They stared at each other, Olivia correctly interpreting his silent message of warning, and then he slashed through the rope binding her to the cart with one swipe of his arm.

"Come with us …" he sniggered "… Sister!"

Olivia managed to glance back as she was led through the trees and saw Walpurga wink encouragement to her as she was lowered out of sight behind the engulfing undergrowth by one of the tinkers. The other licked his lips with a slug-like tongue, his eyes almost popping from his pasty face, as he opened his breeches and slowly disappeared down behind the same screen of green vegetation. The last thing Olivia saw behind her as she was wrenched further into the silent woods was the cart standing alone, as if the two tinkers and Walpurga had never been there.

"'Ere," panted the short fat man after a short distance, "this'll do."

"Please," said Olivia bravely as the two ruffians turned on her. "I am very thirsty. Could I please have a drink of something?"

"On your knees."

Olivia obeyed immediately.

"Thirsty, are you?" said the leader, taking a flask from his pocket and teasing it before her eyes.

"Yes - yes I am." She reached for it with her bound hands.

The men tutted and grinned in unison. "Now, now," said the leader. "Don't forget your manners."

"Please," begged Olivia quietly.

"Beg pardon? Couldn't 'ear you."

"Please," she said desperately. "I need a drink."

"Very well, but first you gotta undo us britches."

Olivia channeled her thoughts on getting a drink from these two, giving them what they wanted, and then escape as soon as the opportunity arose. She fumbled with the buttons of the leader's garment, and then saw to the short fat one. She could feel their erections against her hands as she did so. "Can I drink now?" she asked again.

The flask hovered above her lips. She put out her tongue, but the flask was withdrawn. She leaned forward, drawn by the enticing moisture lingering on the neck.

"Take out us cocks first."

Olivia sank back forlornly on her haunches. "Must I?" she asked, although she knew it was a pointless question.

The leader nodded and the fat man chuckled. "You must."

She reached inside the breeches of first the leader, felt for his organ, closed her fist around the shaft, and guided it out through the opening. She repeated the operation and both men stood with their cocks bobbing before her face.

"Will you let me drink now, please?"

A hand cupped the back of her head. "Put out your tongue," ordered the leader.

Again she obeyed, and was rewarded as a drop of beautifully cool water dripped into her mouth and down her parched throat. She closed her eyes and felt something smooth rest on her tongue. She knew what it was. It slid slowly down and between her open lips. More water was her priority, so she knelt quietly and allowed the rigid column to nudge the back of her throat. She closed her lips around its base and sucked hard.

"Fuckin' 'ell," she heard the leader croak. "The wench sure knows 'ow t'use 'er mouth." She could hear the fat man panting in anticipation of testing her ability for himself.

The intruder retreated, and she was rewarded with another swig of water. Then the fat man eagerly took his turn in her mouth, and wholeheartedly agreed with the opinion of his leader. This procedure was repeated until they decided Olivia was suitably replenished with liquid sustenance.

Feeling humiliated by the behaviour of the pair, but physically better for the generous imbibe, Olivia decided it was time to create a little luck of her own. Walpurga would probably be close to wearing her captors down and overpowering them by now, so she wanted to be ready to make her move also. Unfortunately the two repugnant men, inadvertently or otherwise, were one step ahead of her, and just when she thought she was winning their confidence the fat one abruptly dashed her rising hopes.

"I don't trust this 'un," he said. "She d'look sly to me. A vixen's eyes if ever I seed any."

"I don't reckon she be any problem, but ..."

Olivia looked up and saw a wicked signal pass between the two. Before she could defend herself she was hauled to her feet, her arms hoisted above her head, and she was hung from the stump of a dead and rotting branch by the rope which bound her wrists. Her arms wrenched in their sockets and her toes just swept the ground. She fought back the desire to scream at the two, knowing it would only heighten their enjoyment and possibly even drive them on to more severe lengths. Endure, she told herself, although any chances of escaping with or without Walpurga had just taken a serious setback.

The leader appeared in front of her, his erection twitching more than ever. He stepped close and without further ado latched onto her stretched nipples like a limpet. His toothless gums nibbled them and his saliva dribbled down her taut breasts and belly. She felt the fat one cup and squeeze her bottom. Hands lifted her thighs and wrapped them around the waist of the leader. At least this took the strain off her poor arms. His thickness nudged at her moist opening. Despite Olivia's predicament her insides knotted with excitement, and she moaned as the man slid into her. The branch creaked, and she hoped it would sustain the weight until she had reached her goal. Her buttocks were prised open and the fat man stabbed at her from behind. This was not possible. Surely not. But yes, he too entered her body and she was impaled between the two ruffians. Olivia loved it.

The two clumsy men found it difficult to set up a satisfactory rhythm. They even started arguing and cursing the others inadequacies and bad sense of timing, but Olivia was oblivious to it all. Their stilted movements unwittingly pleased her greatly, and her head lolled forward onto the shoulder of the leader. Her climax was fast approaching. She squeezed and milked the two rigid givers of such pleasure. The men forgot their wrangles and stared at each other with expressions of imbecilic stupidity. They flooded Olivia simultaneously, and their copious spendings triggered her own wonderful orgasm. The three writhed together. Olivia whimpered beautifully, and the men gawked foolishly.

By the time they rejoined the cart Walpurga was again tied to the tailgate and her two assailants sat on the back grinning broadly.

"This'n tried t'make a run for it!" jeered one of them to the approaching party.

"Yeah," confirmed the other. "Silly mare. Mus' fink we was stupid!"

The feeble attempt to escape had failed miserably, but Olivia still glowed in the aftermath of her orgasm. Indeed,

Walpurga also looked replete and oblivious to the tinkers' continuing uncouth comments about her extremely accommodating sexual prowess. The leader and the fat man clambered back up onto the cart and off they set once again, in the same direction as before.

The party now traveled in silence, each member with their own thoughts. Only when they forded the stream did anyone speak.

"We're here," said the leader gruffly.

The two captives looked up at the foreboding grey walls. They heard the sound of a window being opened and a shrill cry.

"They're back!"

CHAPTER FIFTEEN

Olivia and Walpurga stood side by side in the private chambers of the Abbess. Nothing disturbed the stillness except an old clock ticking quietly over a yawning fireplace. They were clothed in short dresses of thin muslin, wrapped around their bodies and reaching only to the tops of their thighs. Walpurga stared defiantly at the wall, fuming at their betrayal. After all they had endured, the tinkers had handed them straight back for a sovereign apiece. Olivia gazed sadly at the floor. It had not yet sunk in that she was back in the convent.

The Abbess had had them brought directly to her apartment. She sat quietly behind her desk, her hands clasped together on its polished surface. Just beside her stood the Mistress, fingertips massaging her temples. Her eyes were closed as if she were in deep and troubled thought.

"I am surprised at you, Walpurga," the Abbess said at length. "You must have known that sooner or later you would be caught. There is no escape from this convent. No matter where you go, or where you hide, I shall find you. Every road and every vehicle that travels upon them leads back here - eventually. Holland, I can understand. She was unaware of how far my arms reach, and was probably easily led. But you have no excuses."

Olivia kept her head bowed, not daring to look into the penetrating and accusatory eyes. She had realized a while ago that she was a prisoner, but had never believed that the confines of the prison could extend so far and wide.

"Take off those dresses."

They both obeyed without question. The muslin floated silently to the floor. Olivia put her hands over her nudity. In contrast Walpurga stood insolently, arms hanging by her sides.

The Mistress, without being told, went to a cabinet and returned with a book which she laid on the desk before the Abbess. They both flicked through the pages, silently studying a host of beautifully illustrated paintings done long, long ago, but still as fresh as ever.

"To tell the truth," the Abbess eventually looked up and said, "the pair of you ought to be racked and flogged, or put to the wheel. But I will make an exception, just this once."

"Thank you Abbess," said Olivia.

Walpurga said nothing.

The Abbess closed the book with a thump and leaned back in her chair, her chin resting on steepled fingers.

"Will the punishment be carried out immediately?" the Mistress asked with a cruel hint of eagerness in her voice.

"Good justice is swift justice. Have them prepared at

once, and assemble the convent in the outer bailey. Have the tinkers gone yet?"

"They are having breakfast, Reverend Mother."

"Retain their services."

And she dismissed both nuns and Novitiate Mistress with a wave of her hand.

CHAPTER SIXTEEN

The Mistress followed the two naked miscreants in single file and herded them to a building close to the herbarium where Sister Lupa was busy manufacturing more of her potions.

"The Abbess is very disappointed with you both," she said, ushering them through the door. "Especially with you, Olivia. And you being so close to the ceremony."

"What ceremony?" Olivia ventured for the first time since her return.

"The ceremony that would have brought you out of your novitiate and into our order as a nun. You were doing so well, and were so near."

They appeared to be in a paint shop of some sort, with pots, kettles, and brushes everywhere.

"You mean, all this suffering and abuse is leading to my being here for the rest of my life?"

The Mistress lifted a pot of paint from a hook and put it on the bench.

"You were selected for our order from the moment you left your home in London. In fact, you were selected before then, but we had to await the right moment. I'd have thought you would have realized that by now and stopped all this foolishness."

Walpurga laughed with derision. "That's why I had to get you away from here before the ceremony -"

"Silence!" snapped the Mistress. "You, Walpurga, have done enough damage for one day. It's all thanks to your stupidity that Holland is in this predicament in the first place." She paused a moment to see whether there were to be any further recusant outbursts, and when satisfied there were not, she took a stick and stirred the pot of bright red paint.

Olivia watched, half distracted by everything she'd heard and the plethora of thoughts spinning in her head. At last the truth was out. All these rituals and everything she'd been subjected to were all part of a greater plan, and not so meaningless after all. Her mind went back to the wine she drank in the infirmary, and the subsequent fantasy. Was that an integral part of the plan too? Was that part of her steady progression towards being incarcerated in the convent forever? The more she thought about it, the more intimidated she became. They had been observing her from the start, perhaps lurking in the shadows and watching the night she was thrown out by Rupert. They had been plotting her every move and then making their own. A shudder ran down her spine. Something in the back of her mind stirred, something about Flora, but try as she might she couldn't bring it to the fore.

"There," the Mistress said with satisfaction when the paint had been suitably stirred. "That should be about ready." She selected a brush and dipped it into the pot. "Please bend over, Sister Walpurga."

A surprisingly subdued Walpurga leant against the bench and thrust out her bottom. Olivia watched in disbelief as a large red disc was painted on her right buttock as if she were a beast going to market. Walpurga remained perfectly still while the brush dipped again into the pot and then applied the finishing touches.

"Stay there until dry," the Mistress told her. "Now you, Miss Holland, bend over the bench."

Having seen the new compliant mood of Walpurga, Olivia sensed correctly that similar compliance would be sensible from hereon in.

"Good," said the Mistress when her masterpiece was done and Olivia could feel the paint hardening on her skin. "You stay there until dry too." With that she left the room, and when she returned a few minutes later she had two nuns with her. "You know where to take them," she said with a cruel smile.

The nuns escorted their charges out of the room and guided them, somewhat bizarrely in Olivia's opinion, towards the slaughterhouse.

"Where are you taking us?" Olivia asked of her escort.

"You'll find out soon enough."

"Why have we been painted?"

"Be quiet."

"I want to know why we've been painted," she persisted.

"I said be quiet."

"Say nothing more, Olivia," whispered Walpurga. "You'll only make it worse for us."

They were indeed heading for the slaughterhouse. "Why are you bringing us here?"

"Olivia!" hissed an exasperated Walpurga. "Will you please be quiet!"

"You'd do well to listen to your traitorous friend," said Olivia's escort.

Heat blasted from the open door and Olivia could see a carcass hanging by its hind legs from a hook. They probably weren't going to slit her throat, she knew that, but the thought was there.

Into the steamy atmosphere they went. Olivia had never seen, or wanted to see, the inside of a slaughterhouse, and the place unsettled her greatly.

The butcher was a grossly overweight nun wearing an apron. She came towards the small party wielding a cleaver as if she were about to hack off an arm, but she merely placed it on a bloodied chopping bench and then wiped her hands in a cloth.

"What have we here?" she asked amiably.

The nun holding Olivia let go. Walpurga stood resigned to whatever was in store.

"We need a headdress," one of the nuns said flatly. "Or a skin - whichever you have available."

Olivia's jaw dropped in horror. "What on earth? You can't mean? I'm not dressing up like an animal!"

"Olivia," sighed Walpurga with a degree of patience that was rarely witnessed by the nuns. "Please be quiet."

"You don't have to," said the other nun. "It's only a gesture, something to make it look a little bit more real."

"Make what look a little bit more real?" beseeched Olivia.

"You," answered the nun, moving closer with a suggestive smile.

Olivia didn't like the lecherous glint in her eye, nor the hand that started smoothing her bottom. The nun ran her hand around Olivia's flank, savouring the feel of her silky slim thighs. "Such beautiful legs," she complimented. "And plenty up here, I see."

Olivia let her fondle her breasts. She'd learnt that it was all in the scheme of things; being handled and mauled by anyone whose fancy she happened to attract. Dumb obedience was the law. The nun opened her hand under the breast and cradled it in her palm, lifting the weight, thumbing the nipple.

"I haven't had the pleasure of making your acquaintance before now," she breathed huskily.

Her colleague, inspired by the groping of Olivia, turned to Walpurga. "Open your legs," she ordered.

The defiance that was Walpurga seemed to have mysteriously evaporated. Now she was like a broken mustang. She obediently opened her legs and allowed the nun to feel her. This was a great moment, for just about every nun in the convent had suffered at the hands of Walpurga at some time or other. "Look," the nun gloated, "she's panting already."

The rest of the group saw the blush on Walpurga's dark face. Her lips parted and she breathed in short, shallow gasps.

"Make her suck you," the nun teasing Olivia said without interrupting her own caresses.

"You heard. On your knees."

Olivia watched in disbelief as Walpurga dropped to the sawdust-covered floor. Where was that spirit of leadership and strength that had almost freed them? Where was that boldness of heart that might, just might, have inspired Olivia to follow wherever she led?

"Good girl," patronized the nun, patting the top of Walpurga's head. "Now, lift my habit."

Walpurga took hold of the hem and rolled it up to her knees. There she stopped and hesitated, as if fighting a conflict with her own inner-self.

"Higher," goaded the nun. "Right up to my waist."

A bare pair of white thighs and buttocks came into view, the faint weals of the nun's most recent flogging showed in pale stripes across the cheeks. Walpurga folded the material into a plait and knotted it. The nun positioned herself closer until her pubic mound was level with Walpurga's face. She spread her feet and shot a victorious glance at her grinning colleague and then at the butcher. "Shall I?" she asked.

Her colleagues nodded enthusiastically. "You'll have to hurry though, they're gathering in the bailey."

Olivia became aware of footsteps and excited chatter moving past outside.

Walpurga's escort pulled the beautiful dark face between her spread legs aggressively. "Lick me!" she snapped. "And be quick about it!"

Olivia saw Walpurga angle her head slightly and stroke up the backs of the nun's thighs to tightly grip her buttocks. She saw the soft flesh whiten as the dark fingers squeezed into it. The nun shuffled and squirmed. Olivia heard her sharp intake of breath and watched her breasts push forward beneath the habit, her nipples clearly visible.

"Ahhh, that feels good," sighed the nun. "I always swore I'd have you do this to me one day. How does it feel to be the submissive for once, you bitch?"

Olivia was more than used to this sort of behaviour by now, but the fact that Walpurga was the recipient made it difficult to accept. Was it an indication of the successfulness of the training here that even the strongest-willed and most defiant of nuns could be reduced to such a pitiful degree of compliance?

Walpurga's head rocked on her shoulders and her face burrowed into the thick thatch. Was she enjoying this new role? Judging by the nun, who whimpered and clutched the wall for support, she was extremely good at it.

Olivia's escort resumed her fondling; her hands imitating those on her companion's bottom. "D'you see how easy it is when you do as you're told?" she panted.

Olivia nodded.

"And are you going to do as you're told from now on?"

She nodded again.

"That's a *good* girl," the nun enthused like an auntie who had just received a commitment from a child to be on its best behaviour while its parents are away. She kissed Olivia deeply. "I'm Sister Alice," she whispered as she broke away. "I'm mistress of the baths."

"Oh … well …" Olivia really had little to say; she was totally disorientated and quietly aroused.

"The baths are beneath the refectory," Sister Alice continued seductively. "You've never been there?"

Olivia shook her head vaguely.

The nun crouching over Walpurga's busy mouth and supported by the wall began to mumble about the imminent arrival of her climax.

"No, I've never been there," Olivia suddenly replied as though only just hearing the question for the first time.

"Then you must come and visit me. Let me bathe you when the entertainment is over. You'll need a nice relaxing wash."

Olivia wasn't really listening again. Sister Alice gently kissed her cheek and licked down to her throat. Olivia felt dreamy. Surreptitious fingers stroked lightly between her legs. Her stomach churned. Her eyes remained fixed on the kneeling Walpurga and her writhing escort. "You're wet," she heard Sister Alice whisper through a haze of conflicting emotions. Her legs felt weak, and she did nothing to resist when Sister Alice backed her against a rough wall beneath a shadowy arch. "Open your legs," she heard from somewhere, and obeyed automatically; responding to an overwhelming desire that was impossible to ignore. As the fingers toyed with her nether-lips she peered over their owner's shoulder and saw the other nun shaking so violently over Walpurga that the butcher was now supporting her in conjunction with the wall. Olivia whimpered for release as her own pleasure mounted.

"Come to the baths afterwards," Sister Alice insisted as she pulled away, much to Olivia's despair.

"Please ..." she begged softly.

"Later," promised Sister Alice. "I'll enjoy you later."

The butcher handed Olivia a small triangle of soft brown leather with cords attached to each corner. Olivia held it up. "What am I supposed to do with this?" she asked with genuine bewilderment.

"Wear it, of course," said Sister Alice. She took it and passed two of the cords around Olivia's waist and tied them behind her back. The cord that hung down at the front was passed between her legs and up through her bottom crease, leaving the buttocks - and more importantly the red mark - completely exposed. This length was tied to the other two. The rude piece of skin was only just large enough to cover her mound, leaving her flanks bare. The butcher then brought a strip of the same leather, plaited and thick at one end and tapering to a point at the other. Olivia stood still while it was tied to the cords over her rump, not unlike a tail. Meanwhile Walpurga was similarly dressed.

"May I ask, what is the purpose of this?" Olivia said, twisting her neck to look down at the tail trailing between her buttocks.

"You'll see, all in good time. Now put this on," beamed the butcher as she fastened an iron shackle to Olivia's wrist. The short chain leading from it was taken to Walpurga and the shackle on the other end likewise fastened.

"Is everything ready?" asked Sister Alice.

"It is," confirmed the butcher, and with that the two were led from the slaughterhouse.

"What's going on?" whispered Olivia fearfully.

Walpurga shook her head. "I'm not sure. Something the Abbess has dreamed up to punish us for running away."

They were directed along the cobbled alleyway and into the outer bailey. The whole convent had assembled at the verges of the lawn and politely applauded when Olivia and Walpurga emerged from the arch. The Abbess was seated on a high-backed chair sipping a glass of wine. Sister Alice led the two miscreants into the centre of the throng and hastily left them, bemused and staring all around.

"I still don't understand," Olivia moaned unhappily.

Walpurga swallowed hard. "I do now ... look up."

Olivia followed her gaze. "Oh my God."

The tinkers had not gone on their way, but were positioned at various points around the quadrangle and were at that moment slotting arrows into bows.

"They're going to kill us!" Olivia shrieked in disbelief. "They're going to shoot us down like animals!"

"It's a lesson," Walpurga said with surprising calm. "A warning to everybody else."

Olivia knew that in the brothels of London whores were often costumed for their rich clients; sometimes as young girls, sometimes made to run around a drawing-room on all fours saddled and bridled like mares - but never as animals hunted with real weapons! Then she realized why her bottom had been painted. She had become a living target! The tinkers would shoot at her as she ran around the lawn in a hopeless search for cover. Had the Abbess gone mad?!

Olivia suddenly had the urge to cross herself; something she had not done for a very long time, but something which now seemed the right thing to do.

The Abbess finished her goblet of wine and settled more comfortably on her throne. A footstool was brought and one of the nuns obediently lifted her feet and placed them on the fabric. Then the Abbess nodded.

The first arrow landed between Walpurga's open legs

and she sprang into the air dragging Olivia after her. Together they fell to the ground, rolling on top of each other, a thrashing confusion of shrieks and naked limbs. They froze in terror, Walpurga on her back and Olivia crouched over her, bare bottom angled upwards. Another arrow sailed harmlessly over their heads and broke in half as it struck the grass. The next whistled closely past Olivia's head. She could feel the rush of air waft her hair.

"Quick, get off me!" Walpurga panicked. "We must keep moving!"

Olivia was up on her feet in a flash, zigzagging across the grass with Walpurga dodging the next volley. Joint-preservation had taken over. Olivia turned an abrupt angle, avoiding an arrow which almost struck her chest. She jerked on the chain and fell. Walpurga kept running, using her immense strength and adrenaline to drag Olivia behind her across the damp grass. The walls reverberated from wild shrieks of laughter as Walpurga tripped and fell. Now it was Olivia who was up on her feet and pulling at the chain.

"Get up!" she screamed over all the commotion. "You must get up!"

Walpurga struggled to her feet and then, with a burst of her long legs, ran swiftly to the other side of the lawn. Olivia managed to follow behind, hopping over the arrows that shot between them.

In their combined panic it had not yet registered that instead of spearing the ground the arrows were merely skidding off it. Neither did they appreciate what a splendid sight they made leaping and twisting in all directions.

The tinkers were whooping and shouting their glee at participating in such entertainment. The leader had toyed with the prey for long enough and was determined to make his mark. He placed an arrow against the string of his bow and drew back, touched his lips to the flight, waited for the right moment, aimed at the red circle on Olivia's superb bottom, held his breath to minimize the movement in his aiming arm, and released.

There was no way Olivia could possibly see or hear the projectile coming. She stooped with her hands resting on her trembling knees, air rasping from her lungs. The arrow struck the red target ferociously and sent her yelping and sprawling head over heels. The chain wrapped around her arm and wrenched her shoulder. The leading tinker cheered his successful strike.

"Are you all right?!" Walpurga lay panting beside her, and then she too howled as an arrow glanced off her vulnerable buttock. Another whistled into her back and one hit Olivia on the back of the head. They curled into tight balls and tried to protect each other with their arms. The onslaught was now relentless. Olivia rolled over in time to see Walpurga yell in agony as she received another on the side of her thigh. Then Olivia was hit simultaneously on her bottom and between the shoulder-blades. The tinkers were firing and reloading at a frenetic rate.

"The arrows aren't real!" Walpurga snarled. "That bitch the Abbess is playing games with us!"

"It's a painful game!" wailed Olivia. She uncurled and was struck on the breast. The arrow deflected away and Walpurga snatched it from the grass. On the tip where a barbed head should have been was a wad of cloth, hard enough to sting but not able to wound.

Suddenly the attack was over. Olivia hid her face in her hands and burst into tears. It wasn't so much the relief that she was still alive as the humiliation of being hunted like an animal, jeered and laughed at as she screamed in desperation. When she struggled to her wobbly feet the skin fell away and left her completely naked. A cheer roared from the archers and a polite applause rose from the nuns.

At a command from the Abbess Walpurga took off her own covering and they stood together naked and chained.

"Approach me," commanded the Abbess with a control that was not a shout yet was clear enough for all present to hear. As she studied the two pitiful creatures before her the Mistress handed her another goblet of wine.

"I hope you have both gained a valuable lesson from this," she said after taking a sip. "In addition to the humiliation of having your bottoms shot at in public, you have also provided the whole convent with some light-hearted entertainment, the purpose of which was to emphasize my power over you and your total submission to me."

Olivia choked back a sob.

"Well, do you have anything to say for yourselves?"

"I understand now, Reverend Mother," Olivia mumbled.

"And you, Walpurga?"

Walpurga nodded.

"And you will not go running off again?"

They both looked down at the grass and shook their heads.

"I will accept your rules," Olivia added without being prompted.

"Very good," smiled the Abbess. "But if you had accepted them in the first place you would have spared yourself a great deal of anguish and trouble. Our rituals were not inflicted upon you merely for the sake of doing so, but to educate you into the secrets of our order. I trust you have now realized that."

Olivia had realized a lot in the past few hours. She had realized there was little chance of escape from the convent. She had realized the Abbess was always one step ahead of all her nuns, and could deliver the appropriate punishment that would, in the end, crush all resistance.

"I shall be obedient from now on, Reverend Mother." At that moment Olivia felt quite sincere in what she was saying. "I shall do whatever is required of me."

"With each passing day, Olivia, you are becoming more and more prepared, and soon, at the ceremony, you will understand the true purpose of our rites. You will learn to love your punishment. You will beg to feel the cut of the whip." With that the Abbess rose and drifted serenely from the arena.

The shackles were removed from the hapless pair and a pail of freezing water thrown over them as the murmuring onlookers began to disperse.

"Now gather up the arrows and return them to the tinkers," the Mistress ordered. "And be thankful you were not put to the wheel."

CHAPTER SEVENTEEN

Bedraggled and deflated Olivia returned alone to her cell to find Sister Letitia waiting for her with a collar and chain.

"I hope you have learned your lesson," the nun said, repeating her Abbess.

"I have, and no thanks to you," Olivia said unhappily.

"What do you mean?"

"You know very well what I mean. If I hadn't met you at that damned station I wouldn't be here now."

"Alas, my dear, you did meet me, and you are here. Now turn around and face the wall."

"Please ..." sighed Olivia, "I just want to lie down and rest for a while."

"You can rest all you like after I've put your collar on."

"Why must you?" sobbed Olivia.

"Because the Abbess wishes it."

"But I promised I wouldn't run away again."

"Saying and doing are two very different things," said Sister Letitia. "Now will you do as you're told, or shall I report you?"

Olivia just couldn't be bothered with all the trouble that might bring. She was too tired and too numb to argue. She faced the wall with her arms by her sides and allowed Sister Letitia to slip the collar around her throat and fasten it at the nape. It was made of leather and fitted with a ring at the side.

"Give me the chain," Sister Letitia said, wriggling the collar to make sure it was a snug fit.

Olivia picked the chain off the cot and gave it to the nun whilst looking longingly through the barred window at the rolling windswept meadows beyond the foreboding walls. She recalled something Walpurga had said that had been nagging her subconscious ever since. "Is there a nun here called Flora?" she asked carefully.

There was a long tense silence.

"Why do you ask?"

She detected a hostility in Sister Letitia's response. "I - I just wondered."

Sister Letitia slipped the chain through the ring and clicked a small brass padlock. "Flora? No, there's no Flora here."

Olivia must have misheard Walpurga in the first place. Perhaps she'd said Dora. Or perhaps it had never even been mentioned at all. Olivia just didn't know what to think any more. She slumped wearily onto the cot, and the free end of the chain was fastened to the wall behind her.

"How long am I to be kept like this?" she asked.

Sister Letitia shrugged. "Until the Abbess decides otherwise." She regarded her charge with a satisfied smile. "I'd get some rest if I were you. Sister Alice will be ready for you soon."

"Sister Alice?"

"Apparently you've promised to have a bath with her."

"I didn't promise anything."

"Pardon?"

"... I'm looking forward to it ..." Olivia was learning.

CHAPTER EIGHTEEN

Sister Alysoun stood beside the rack in the punishment room dressed in only a short pale cream shift. She eyed the fearful piece of equipment with dread.

"How is it you failed to lock the water-gate, Sister Alysoun?" the Mistress asked calmly.

Sister Alysoun looked up at her interrogator and wrung her hands. "I - I thought it was locked, Mistress."

"But it wasn't, was it? Or how else would Walpurga and the new girl find their way through the culvert?"

"I don't know, Mistress."

"Did they saw their way through the bars?" She laughed sardonically, and the two attendant nuns behind her chuckled dutifully.

Sister Alysoun looked down again in agitation and fiddled with the hem of her shift. "No, Mistress, they didn't."

"Well?"

"I was late for compline, Mistress."

"Don't take me for a fool, Sister Alysoun. Compline is the last service in the chapel after supper. It was your job to close the gate long before that. You're lying again."

Sister Alysoun grit her teeth. She knew the Mistress would not relent until the truth was out. "I forgot," she whispered.

"Speak up - what did you say?"

"I forgot, Mistress."

"And nearly lost us two Sisters. If it hadn't been for that bunch of filthy tinkers and the foresight of the Abbess to deploy them in the woods your punishment would have been much more severe."

"Yes, Mistress."

"Well," sighed the Mistress like a disappointed teacher, "what shall I do with you? The rack or the cross? You decide."

It was the lesser of two utterly awful evils. Sister Alysoun eyed the two attendant nuns in their thin yellow punishment tunics. They were tall and robust, and although friends of hers, she knew there would be no compassion shown. Their powerful arms could turn the rollers of the rack as easily as winding water from the well.

"The cross," she eventually muttered.

"Very good. Then walk to it and position yourself in readiness."

Sister Alysoun moved across the dank room with the two attendant nuns close behind. The oak cross was conventional in appearance, about man height and suspended on thick chains. It didn't move when she stood with her back against it.

"Raise your arms," the Mistress continued coldly. She had good reason for wanting to punish wretched Sister Alysoun. When the Abbess heard that Walpurga and Olivia had fled the convent she had threatened to reduce the Mistress to the rank of an ordinary nun. That was a fate worse then any rack or whip, and not to be even contemplated. The whole convent would have tormented her, for there was many a score to settle.

Sister Alysoun lifted her arms to the crossbeam and closed her eyes. She knew only too well what to expect; all the nuns were aware of the perils of the punishment room.

"Hold still," instructed one of the nuns as they locked her arms into a number of hinged iron shackles attached at intervals to the crossbeam.

"Shall we secure her fully, Mistress?" one of the nun's asked.

"Oh yes, I think so," she mused, enjoying the sight of the pale shift stretched tightly over her victim's inviting breasts. "I want Sister Alysoun to feel the full benefit of the cross."

The nuns set about their task, and were soon sweating heavily from their studious efforts. Rivulets of perspiration also trickled down between Sister Alysoun's cleavage and disappeared inside her damp tunic which stuck to every contour of her luscious body, making her appear almost naked.

The attendants took a heavy chain and wrapped it around her, over her shoulders, behind the vertical beam, and back round just beneath her breasts. She was squeezed against the beam and groaned from the discomfort. The links dug into her soft flesh and lifted her breasts towards the passive Mistress.

One of the nuns then bent to lock her ankles into the two iron shackles at the base of the beam while the other went to a water-barrel and took a long refreshing drink. She passed the metal mug to her companion, who made a great show of savouring the cool liquid right in front of Sister Alysoun, and then cruelly dribbled that which she didn't drink onto the dusty floor. Sister Alysoun whimpered at the unnecessary teasing.

"Blindfold her," ordered the Mistress.

"Oh please don't," pleaded Sister Alysoun. "I hate being in the dark."

"Be quiet!" snapped the Mistress angrily, and then addressing the two nuns calmly said again: "Blindfold her."

Sister Alysoun knew better than to protest any further, and despite her anguish she made not another sound as the nuns wrapped a black cloth over her eyes and knotted it tightly at the back of her head.

"She is ready, Mistress," said one of them. "Shall we whip her now?"

"No," came the emphatic reply. "I shall whip her." The Mistress selected a long bullwhip from a wall-rack and moved close enough to the helpless victim that she could smell her fear. She allowed the whip to uncoil and snake out on the stone floor. The two nuns backed respectfully away to give their superior enough room in which to operate; neither of them would have swapped places with poor Sister Alysoun at that moment. With a casual expertise the Mistress flicked her arm and the whip came alive. It cracked through the sticky air and Sister Alysoun flinched in her bonds. Her arm and thigh muscles tensed and her stomach hollowed. The wooden cross creaked from her sudden movement and the metal links chinked and scraped together. The Mistress stepped closer until her face almost touched Sister Alysoun's.

"Did you hear that?" she whispered flatly.

Sister Alysoun nodded frantically. "Yes Mistress. Yes, I heard it."

The two nuns strained unsuccessfully to hear the hushed exchange.

The Mistress turned the whip and held the tip of the leather plaited handle against Sister Alysoun's soft lips. "Do you feel that?" she continued.

"Yes Mistress, I feel it."

The Mistress loved the way the nun's chin trembled. She angled the handle and pushed it between her lips and into her mouth. "Suck," she insisted.

"I'm not really going to whip you now, Sister Alysoun." She slipped the wetted handle from her moist mouth, over her chin, and down her throat to her breasts. It stroked to and fro between her deep cleavage, and then slowly moved to her nipples where it rubbed in small circles. "Say thank you." Although her tone was almost compassionate, the words carried an immensely sinister threat.

"Thank you, Mistress," blurted Sister Alysoun, the tension almost unbearable for her.

The whip moved on, down over the chain and across her flat stomach. The Mistress wasn't about to waste those gloriously erect nipples, and she pinched them through the thin wet tunic between finger and thumb, and listened contentedly to Sister Alysoun's tormented groans.

"No, I'm not going to whip you now," she continued. "That pleasure will be saved for someone else. You will be whipped at the ceremony."

"Mistress?"

The two watching nuns were transfixed by the scene. They watched the whip handle nudge between quivering thighs, lift the hem of the tunic, pause, and then rise slowly upwards and disappear from view. The sweating body on the cross went rigid. The Mistress was still talking softly. Suddenly she kissed Sister Alysoun long and hard on the lips, and then stepped back. The length of leather dangled obscenely from the bound nun and twitched on the floor as her vagina spasmed around the unwelcome handle.

The Mistress cackled her delight. "Come with me," she said loudly to the two watching nun's, her raised voice suddenly breaking the spell which hung over the gruesome room. "We'll leave our young friend here alone for a while to consider the consequences of her wholly unacceptable oversight."

The two nuns looked uneasily at each other as they locked the heavy wooden door and followed their cackling Mistress along the dark passageway to the main convent.

CHAPTER NINETEEN

The baths had existed since the time of the original castle. Far below ground they were fed from a hot spring. Steaming water gushed from a culvert and into a huge lead-lined basin, large enough to accommodate the entire inhabitants of the convent.

Sister Alice had been waiting, and immediately lay Olivia on a bench and set about massaging oils into her body, soothing any aches and pains until they had all but disappeared. Then for some inexplicable reason she departed, telling Olivia to immerse herself in the water to help the oils soak into her skin and really do their work. Olivia swam underwater to the other side of the pool and back again, her long hair trailing behind like a dark, shimmering cloak. It was here that the trials and tribulations of the world were forgotten.

There were no more than a dozen or so other nuns in the chamber. It was lit by torches let into alcoves. They created a dreamlike, ruddy effect as if the water were on fire. In half-shadow some of the nuns padded naked around the perimeter. Some languished and caressed each other, and others just whispered the gossip of the convent. Olivia was largely ignored as she floated on the surface of the soft water, moving her hands and feet in gentle waves.

She drifted to the far side of the basin where it was almost dark. Here the ceiling was lower and the basin narrowed to little more than a body's width.

"Alice?" she murmured, aware of another presence but without opening her eyes.

Hands gripped her shoulders and began to massage them beautifully, working the thumbs along the top of the blades and into the crook of her neck. It seemed a world away from being chased and hunted around the quadrangle like an animal.

The hands slipped furtively from her shoulders and covered her breasts. It felt wonderful. They embraced them and studiously teased the nipples. They massaged in hypnotic circles. A deep purr escaped Olivia's lips; so good did it feel to be pampered.

"What have I done to deserve this?" she whispered.

"What have you done? You have been very patient. It's the least I can do."

The voice was not that of Alice, but from the past. A voice she had not heard for a long time. But it couldn't be - she was dreaming; the soothing atmosphere of the chamber making her imagine things. The hands left her breasts and went under her shoulders. The unseen person slipped off the edge of the pool and into the gently lapping water behind her. Olivia was half-lifted and then settled back between a pair of lovely white thighs which floated to the surface on either side of her. Her head rested on a yielding cushion of milky breasts as they drifted further into the shadows. Fingers returned to tease her nipples, and others worked their way down to her velvet fleece.

"Open your mouth," the voice breathed in her ear.

Olivia obeyed without question, so naturally close did she feel to this mystery partner, and sucked on the fingertips that slipped unhindered between her parted lips. Again something stirred in the distant recesses of her mind - and again she dismissed it as ridiculous. She moaned when one of the mischievous fingers burrowed between her labia and instantly located her most sensitive spot.

"Good?"

"Hmm."

"Shall I continue?"

Olivia couldn't remember the last time she had been shown such genuine consideration. What else could she do but nod her desire?

The fingers in her mouth she caressed with her tongue, while the others slipped gently inside her waiting sex, seeking only to give the ultimate satisfaction.

"You feel good," Olivia gasped as her clitoris responded to the intimate coaxing.

"And your nipples - would you like me to touch your nipples again?" The voice was so low she could barely hear it above the rippling water and the distant whispers and giggles from the other nuns on the opposite side of the chamber.

"Yes please. Do anything you like to me."

The anonymous hands moved together, one teasing her towards orgasm, the other relaxing around her nipples, thumbing and rolling the erect teats. Olivia looked dreamily at her silky-wet breasts rising out of the water like twin islands.

"When did you last feel this good?"

Olivia sighed. "Oh, not for a long time. Not since I ..." She caught her breath as her juices began to seep over the gliding fingers.

"When you ..?"

"When I was in a House of Correction. I had a friend there. We met again in London ... and ..."

The hand spread across Olivia's whole breast and squeezed it hard. The pain was both agonizing and deeply satisfying. Slowly her back arched in the lap of her lover. Her legs floated on the scented surface.

"You were telling me about your friend," the voice coaxed in her ear.

Olivia took a deep breath and tried to concentrate. "We were in London … she rescued me from a brothel ..."

The expert hands continued to work their magic. Olivia shivered. Her legs floated wider.

"Tell me about the brothel."

"It was a horrible place. I had to dress up and do things for the customers."

"You didn't like that?"

"No, not really. I tried to please them, but usually they would spank me afterwards."

"Didn't you like being spanked?"

Olivia frowned and tried to remember just how she had felt. "I - I don't know. It didn't really hurt - I suppose."

"Shall I spank you now?"

Lips fluttered against Olivia's ear as the seductive voice toyed with her. She really didn't know what she wanted, but the thought of a wet palm stinging her wet bottom knotted her stomach. She stared at the bricks overhead, and then at the ruddy glow beyond the secluded arch. There was nobody close to observe what they were doing.

"If you would like to," she consented. "But please don't hurt me too much. It's so lovely and peaceful here."

"You like the convent then?"

"The convent, no. But the baths, yes. I like it here."

"If you relax and accept, you might grow to like the convent. Everyone is happy here. I couldn't live anywhere else."

"What were you outside?"

"Turn over and let me spank you."

The unknown nun slithered back onto a stone ledge-seat which just broke the surface at the edge of the pool. Olivia closed her eyes, not wanting to break the mystical spell. She twisted and luxuriated in the feel of the warm swirling water as she lay over a pair of slippery thighs. Her tummy rested comfortably on the smooth flesh. Her legs rested on the seat on one side of the nun, and her forehead rested on her folded arms on the other.

"Are you ready?"

Olivia nodded, and swooned as the first wet slap landed on her raised buttocks. It stung a little more than she expected - but it was nice. The spanking continued, but it was tender - without malice. The sound of flesh hitting flesh reverberated lightly off the low arch.

"Your delightful bottom is made for smacking."

"Thank you," Olivia whispered stupidly. She squirmed a little on the lap, but an arm lay across her back and pinned her in place. The hand continued to fall rhythmically until Olivia's excitement threatened to burst, and then it stopped and deftly pushed its way between her buttocks.

"Are any of the other nuns watching us?" she mumbled into her arm.

"One or two."

"They won't stop us, will they?"

The mystery nun chuckled softly and stroked Olivia's wet hair. "They wouldn't dare."

"Are you keeping me all to yourself?"

"Yes - for a while."

A finger slipped into Olivia's wetness again and she gasped, "Please let me come."

"In a moment, my little treasure."

The weight of the arm left her back, and Olivia felt her buttocks being prised apart. The lubricated finger retreated from her sex and then rubbed gently around her rear entrance. She held her breath; the nun's intent was clear - even through her swirling emotions. Olivia whimpered. The finger eased down. There was a slight resistance, and then Olivia's bottom opened and welcomed the rude intrusion.

Both women were silent now, save for their slow breathing. The free hand patted Olivia's cheeks and moulded them around the buried digit. The nun leaned down and kissed the nape of Olivia's neck, sending thrilling ripples down her spine. Olivia purred and writhed like a kitten.

"Keep still, Miss Holland," admonished the secret nun kindly. "Or I'll have to send you straight back to the brothel, and I won't be there to rescue you."

Olivia froze. Did she know all about that? No. It was impossible. It was a crude threat to make her obey. "Alice," she beseeched, "why are you teasing me? Please make me come. You know I want to. You know I'm close."

The nun whispered softly, "Turn over, Olivia."

For a full minute Olivia stared incredulously into the smiling eyes. "But, it - it's impossible!" she stammered at last. "I - I can't believe this! Is it really you?!"

Flora put her arms around Olivia's shoulders and lifted her onto the ledge. "It is me," she cooed like a mother hen, brushing a lock of wet hair from Olivia's furrowed brow.

"But I thought - I mean - the telegram ..."

"I'm afraid that was a trick too."

"But how long have you been here?"

"Ever since I left London. There never was a boarding-house, I made that place up. I knew you were coming, but was told to keep silent."

Olivia wasn't sure whether the tears in her eyes were those of relief or shock. "So all the time you were here, knowing that I was trying to reach you in Ottery."

Flora seated herself more comfortably. She pulled Olivia close, settling her head on her shoulder.

"I couldn't reveal myself, not until you'd passed all the tests. It was part of your training, filling you with false hope, leading you on, seeing how determined you were to escape. You nearly made it, and might have done if Walpurga hadn't led you into the woods."

"That was all a trick too, I suppose."

"No, it wasn't actually. The Abbess was furious when she learned that Walpurga had got you out. Walpurga wanted you for her own, you see. I suppose she was afraid of losing you to me and the Abbess, and so she decided to steal you from us."

Olivia threw her arms around Flora and kissed her throat. She remained quiet in the safe warmth of her friend for a few minutes, but there was so much she needed to know. "What's the purpose of all these spiteful rituals?" she soon gabbled like and inquisitive child. "And what's this mysterious ceremony I keep hearing about?"

"There's nothing mysterious about it," Flora reassured as best she could. "Hundreds of years ago the nuns were evicted from their convent. They settled here, in this empty castle, and the Abbess hid her plate and the sacred books so the order could continue to flourish. But there was one immense problem; how were they to keep -"

"- Recruiting," Olivia interrupted, beginning to understand.

"Precisely. Because the nuns were banished no one would send their daughters to take up the order -"

"- So they resorted to other methods - like having unsuspecting girls abused, robbed, and left naked on the highway to be conveniently picked up and brought here." The stress of recent events fought for release, and tears started to trickle down Olivia's pink cheeks. Flora soothed her with tender kisses, and Olivia sniffled an apology for her outburst and silly emotions.

"Now, now then," Flora whispered kindly. "It's not all as bad as it may seem. You easily exceeded expectations. You're almost one of us now - a nun in the order of saint Dulcinea. After the ceremony you will be a confirmed Dulcinite." She said it with such pride and devotion that Olivia was temporarily lost for words.

"What does 'Spiritus Licentia Copulatum' mean?" she asked suddenly.

"It's Latin. It means, spiritual freedom to act without restraint." She laughed. "In plain English, it means we can do just what we like with each other, providing the rules are obeyed."

"And no one has any say in who sleeps with them?"

"You'll get used to it," Flora assured quietly.

Olivia thought she would never get used to indulging in sexual practices with a whole castle full of frustrated women, with the threat of being punished if she refused them the privilege. The more Flora told her the less she liked the idea. It was perfectly clear that once she had been accepted as a Dulcinite she would never again be allowed to set foot outside the walls as a free person.

"What exactly happens during the ceremony?" she asked.

"I am not permitted to tell you. But you will find out soon enough; only a couple of days to go, and then everybody will gather to witness your acceptance into our order. And when you have been accepted life will become much easier. You'll be offered a choice as to your new profession. If I were you, I'd ask to work alongside Sister Lupa the herbalist. Or you could ..."

Olivia stopped listening to Flora's words. She was amazed at how her friend had become so easily influenced against the outside world. Olivia knew it was a race against time. The longer she was there the more like them she would become, rather like a convict or a whore who prefer a prison or a brothel because they offer a security that is difficult to find in the harshness of day to day existence outside.

"The herbalist will suit me nicely," she said when she became aware her friend had stopped talking. She lowered her lips to the erect nipple which quivered beneath her breath, wondering if the drug she was sure had been put in her wine could be administered to the whole convent.

CHAPTER TWENTY

Now that she had found her old friend Flora, Olivia was thrown into even worse confusion. She had run away from London hoping to start a new life, but all her plans had been thwarted. She did not want to stay in the convent, and she did not want to go crawling back to Rupert. Suddenly she felt more isolated and adrift than at any other time in her life. Perhaps fate had designed it that way. Perhaps she had always been destined to enter the convent of saint Dulcinea, and all her life had been but a preparation for that moment - the moment she was dreading.

"Come in," she called absently in response to the knock at her door.

Flora entered and placed a bundle on the end of the cot, her face radiant. "'Tis time," she beamed, taking Olivia's hand and guiding her to her feet.

"Am I to be naked?"

Flora's smile widened. "Of course not." She indicated

the bundle. "See, I've brought your ceremonial robe."

She unfolded the bundle and joyfully held up the contents. It was virginal white and virtually transparent, full-length and embroidered at the edges with symbols and codes which were meaningless to Olivia. She carefully lifted the diaphanous material and dropped it neatly over Olivia's head. It shimmered and nestled snugly over her statuesque contours. Flora then picked up a black cord from the bundle and wound it tightly around Olivia's waist before knotting it at the front. Then she kissed her friend lightly on both cheeks.

"Look at yourself in the mirror. See how wonderful you are."

The robe was beautifully crafted out of silk, shining and clinging. Her breasts stood out clearly, revealing their firm outline and dark teats. When she moved the material clung like a sleek skin.

"Sit on the stool," said Flora, moving behind the breathtaking vision. "I must do your hair now."

"Where are the older nuns?" Olivia asked suddenly as she sat before the mirror. She could see Flora was taken aback by the unexpected question - she had touched a nerve.

Flora parted Olivia's hair in the middle and brushed until the tresses shone. "Older nuns?" she replied at last, as though with little interest or understanding.

"Yes. Apart from the Abbess and the Mistress and Sister Lupa there doesn't seem to be a woman in here over thirty. Where are the older ones?"

Flora said nothing as she brushed all the more vigorously.

"Where do they go?" Olivia persisted, feeling uneasy at Flora's obvious reluctance to comment.

"You really do ask a lot of questions, my treasure." She tied an embroidered band around Olivia's forehead, using the reflection to adjust it between eyebrows and fringe.

Then she reached down and allowed herself the luxury of holding those glorious breasts for a few seconds, watching her own lucky hands in the mirror, before straightening the robe a fraction so that it opened to reveal the deep cleavage and swept out to the tips of Olivia's shoulders.

"Come - it is time to go."

Flora led her charge through the dim and empty corridors of the convent to the chapel. Outside the great doors Olivia managed to stop her.

"Why won't you tell me about the older nuns?" she asked. "There must be some here."

"You will learn all there is to know in due course," Flora told her firmly. "In the meantime, hold your tongue and do exactly as you're told."

She opened the chapel doors and pushed her dangerously inquisitive young friend inside.

At first Olivia couldn't see anything for the dense incense swirling in clouds from tripods positioned all around the walls. For the past two days after her strange encounter with Flora she had tried to imagine what sort of procedure the ceremony would take. She had imagined it to be like a normal church service; the nuns kneeling and chanting from their prayer books and the Abbess reading from one of the illustrated manuscripts. She had never, however, contemplated a scene like that which greeted her slowly adjusting eyes.

The macabre tableau was lit by torches which sent fantastic shadows dancing grotesquely over the frescos and revealed the white nakedness of the nuns, eyes blazing and bodies quivering with sexual tension. They stood in two lines leading to the altar, an avenue of taut buttocks and erect nipples bathed in sweat. At the end of the avenue, on the raised platform before the altar, stood the Abbess. She was dressed in a shimmering red gown that intimately hugged her curves. Olivia could just about see her through the swirling incense.

The Abbess reached out with both hands and beckoned her forward. She did not want to go. Her feet would not move. Flora gave a gentle prod in the small of her back, and she slowly and reluctantly walked along the writhing human corridor. The naked figures glowed and shimmied in the orange light. Their arms and fingers twisted and snatched, but none touched her.

At the foot of the altar she halted and hesitated, not really knowing what to do next. She was greatly relieved to find Flora still with her.

To Olivia's right, and previously unseen by her, stood the Mistress. She held a silk cushion upon which were balanced a short stout whip and a cane. The Abbess stared deeply into Olivia's wide eyes and nodded once. Immediately Sister Lupa appeared from an archway to Olivia's left, guiding Sister Alysoun to the altar rail. Sister Alysoun wore a blue silk robe which draped from her shoulders right down to the floor. She looked vacant, her eyes soulless. Olivia wanted to ask if she was all right, but knew better than to do such a thing.

Another barely noticeable nod from the Abbess and Sister Lupa, standing behind her charge, reached around and unbuttoned the neck of the blue gown. The frenzied chaos from the congregation suddenly ceased as she peeled it away and revealed Sister Alysoun in breathtaking nudity. A silence hung over the chapel for some moments, and then, as if upon a signal, the chaos resumed.

Olivia was utterly bewildered. She had assumed it was she who would be stripped. Why was Sister Alysoun involved? What on earth was going to happen next? Her attention was drawn back to the Abbess who was raising her arms towards the ceiling.

"Olivia Holland," the Abbess announced in a clear, powerful voice. Again the congregation fell quiet and listened to their leader with absolute adoration. "Since your arrival within our sacred walls you have been disobedient, disrespectful -"

"I have not!" protested Olivia.

"Silence!" stormed the Mistress at the outrageous outburst.

"Thank you, Mistress," said the Abbess, and then started again with a clear look in her eyes that a second interruption would most certainly not be tolerated. "Since your arrival within our sacred walls you have been disobedient, disrespectful, and generally problematic. Lastly, of course, you committed the greatest of sins by trying to leave us without permission."

"I've been punished for that."

"I won't tell you again!" hissed the Mistress.

"Yes, Olivia Holland, you have been punished for that," continued the Abbess smoothly, "but you have not been cleansed."

Poor Olivia was dumbstruck. What on earth was occurring?

"You may speak now," the Abbess prompted. "Have you anything to say for yourself?"

Olivia had nothing to say. These women were going to do exactly as they wished with her, no matter what she said. She shook her head.

"Very well - we shall begin. Choose, Olivia Holland."

"I'm sorry?"

"You must choose whether to use the whip or the cane."

"What must I use them for?"

The Abbess looked with annoyance at the Mistress. "Does the foolish girl mean to try my patience?"

The Mistress stepped forward and handed the cushion to

Flora. "I apologize for her misguided behaviour, Abbess. Allow me." She turned to Olivia. "Sister Alysoun has been found guilty of gross neglect, the consequence of which was your foolish and temporary absence from our order. To safeguard against further transgressions she must be punished. You will see to it. And once the punishment has been concluded you may consider yourself cleansed, and therefore pure."

Olivia looked at the emotionless face of Sister Alysoun. "This is unfair," she uttered. "Sister Alysoun has done nothing against me."

"Nonsense," said the Mistress. "What about your torture in the punishment room?"

"But that has nothing to do with this."

"Perhaps. But you should have thought of that before you selfishly ran off. You should have considered the ramifications of your actions upon those you left behind. It is the rule that when a Sister transgresses by attempting to leave without permission - and it doesn't happen often - those left behind and considered responsible through negligence shall pay."

"Please ... this is ridiculous ..." This was emotional blackmail of the worst kind; that someone innocent should suffer because of her wrongdoing, and that she should have to select the mode of punishment and administer it herself.

"Sister Lupa," said the Mistress. "To the altar rail please."

The herbalist guided the passive Sister Alysoun down to kneel on a waiting footstool. She pushed her shoulders forward until her flat stomach rested over the rail and her bottom was lifted high.

"Abbess," whispered a humble Olivia. "I would rather take the punishment myself. This is not fair."

"Perhaps not," said the Abbess without compassion. "But

you will learn your lesson well. Now, please commence without further delay."

Olivia eyed the ominous looking implements laying on the cushion, and decided the cane looked the lesser of two undoubted evils. She held it gingerly in her fingers. It quivered as she approached the rail. She bent and whispering to Sister Alysoun: "I'm sorry. I would give anything not to do this."

Sister Alysoun said nothing. She just stared at the floor.

"Twelve strokes," commanded the Abbess.

Olivia looked at the bare buttocks waiting for the first strike. They were neat and pale and vulnerable.

The congregation waited in silence ...

A muffled grunt betrayed the scorching pain felt from the first blow. Olivia's stomach churned at the sight of the reddening welt delivered from her own hand. It ran from cheek to cheek. Only where it crossed the narrow cleft was the flesh unmarked.

"Again," demanded the Mistress.

Olivia hated the bespectacled woman with an intensity never before felt. She swept the cane into Sister Alysoun again. But it wasn't the Sister she was thrashing; it was the Mistress. Her victim rocked forward on the rail under the heavy assault. The next blow was for the Abbess. Olivia was swept along within an all-consuming fury. All she could see was the poor bottom and the cane. All she could feel was hatred for the Abbess and the Mistress. Flora too; she was no longer Olivia's friend. She had lured her to this place.

"Enough!" announced the Abbess.

Olivia struck again. Through a red haze she could see nothing but Flora's damned face.

"Enough, I said!"

Olivia's arm swept down again, but was snatched by the

Mistress and halted before it could inflict yet more damage. The cane dropped from her limp fingers and clattered to the stone floor. Sister Alysoun sobbed quietly over the rail.

"Take a good look, Olivia Holland," ordered the Abbess. "See what misery you have inflicted on your fellow."

"Not I," she protested. "You ordered this cruelty."

"And so I shall again if you continue to flout the rules of this convent." She ran her fingers back through her shock of long auburn hair. Her breasts lifted enticingly and Olivia saw the erect nipples send shimmering darts through the red silk. The diaphanous material moulded itself to her elegant hips and clung to her shapely thighs and calves. She was intentionally preening herself before Olivia, and Olivia couldn't deny she was an incredibly sensuous woman. "This part of the ceremony is over," she announced dramatically. "You are cleansed of your past transgressions, Olivia Holland."

From somewhere rose the steady low beat of a drum. A flute joined it, its haunting tune drifting through the swirling gloom. The heady incense wafting from the tripods reduced the naked congregation to a wraithlike mass of gyrating and embracing limbs.

The Abbess stepped down to Olivia and took her hand. Now a different atmosphere prevailed. "Sister Lupa will prepare you," she breathed, and kissed Olivia delicately on the lips.

Sister Lupa put her arms around Olivia's shoulders and steered her to an alcove behind the altar. She opened a waiting glass jar containing a sweetly perfumed ointment. "An oil made from bergamot and lavender," she informed without being asked. "To make you feel at ease … and receptive."

"Receptive?" Olivia asked cautiously, watching the herbalist coat her fingers with a little of the ointment.

"Don't worry," she whispered comfortingly. "Just relax and abandon yourself to the coming pleasures. You are a very lucky girl." She touched her lubricated fingertips gently to the base of Olivia's throat, and allowed them to glide down into her cleavage. The aroma was reassuring as the warm ointment was rubbed into her flesh. The fingertips swept outwards in slowly increasing circles until they slipped beneath the white silk and coated Olivia's already erect nipples. She shuddered and moaned softly. The excitement sparked deep in the pit of her stomach.

"Lucky?" her voice could barely be heard.

"Hush ..." Sister Lupa coaxed gently. "Don't talk any more ..."

Olivia tried to resist the wonderful sensations permeating her breasts and nipples. Her heart beat steadily faster; a persistent throbbing which reverberated through her chest. Gradually the sounds from the chapel evaporated. Olivia's head span. Her attention was glued to Sister Lupa and her wonderful fingers. "Kiss me ..." she couldn't prevent herself from sobbing. "Please, kiss my nipples ..."

The herbalist needed no second invitation. Without hesitation she lowered her head and pressed her lips over the white silk where each delicious bud strained from within. She urged Olivia back against the alcove wall, peeled aside the material and drew an exposed and swollen nipple into her mouth. She flicked her tongue over the tip and nibbled it between her pearly teeth. Olivia inhaled deeply, and her breasts swelled against Sister Lupa's hot face.

"Ooh ..." she moaned, and cupped the back of the herbalist's head to pull her closer and to force yet more of her aching breast into the tantalizing mouth. Her back and bottom squirmed against the cold wall. "Oh ... what are you doing to me?"

By way of an answer Sister Lupa merely cupped and lifted both breasts and sucked on the unattended nipple. The air was heavy with sexual expectation.

"That wicked potion ..." complained Olivia without conviction.

Sister Lupa reached blindly, found the jar, and coated her fingers again. Unseen fumblings, and Olivia felt the silk whispering up her legs. The industrious mouth and tongue never left her nipples. She held her breath. The excitement threatened to burst forth from her chest. Her feet shuffled a little further apart. When the material was gathered around her waist the slick fingers and palm roamed over her thighs and belly. They slipped around and into the valley between her trembling buttocks. A finger pressed and teased over her private entrance, and then returned to coat her wet labia with the wonderful ointment.

"I shall come ..." Olivia sighed. "If you keep doing such lovely things to me I shall come." Her head lolled to one side and through glazed and hooded eyes she saw in the chapel a writhing carpet of nuns making love to each other. "What's happening to me ..?" she pleaded. "I need you to make love to me, Sister Lupa. And I need you to make me come."

As though from the depths of a dream Olivia saw the chapel doors opening through the haze. A recumbent figure was brought in on a sledge to the accompaniment of manic adoration from the congregation.

"The moment has arrived." Sister Lupa kissed her. "You are well prepared." Olivia was enflamed. Her brain pounded to the mayhem all around as the herbalist left the dress in its state of disarray and led her back out and stood with her beside the Abbess.

It took a large group of nuns to lift the marble figure from the sledge and up onto the altar. Olivia gazed upon it with a comfortable sense of serenity. It was obscene - yet beautiful. From its groin there reared a large and lifelike phallus. Her legs quaked and her belly knotted at the promise of it. Its stomach was flat, and where there should have been a broad and masculine chest there rose a pair of beautiful breasts tipped with erect nipples. Olivia wasn't at all shocked; the figure possessed a magical sexual magnetism. The peaceful face was of a woman, wondrously carved with long flowing hair. Olivia knew it was an image of the Abbess who had saved the order from extinction all those centuries ago.

"Sister Lupa," said the Abbess. "If you would be so kind."

Sister Lupa stepped forward with the same glass jar and coated the phallus generously with the sweet ointment. Olivia could hear the slick sound of the herbalist's fingers working up and down the inanimate length and over the flawless helmet. When the herbalist stepped away the phallus glistened proudly.

"Olivia Holland ..." announced the Abbess over the noise of the throng. "Step forward, Olivia Holland ..."

The Mistress took Olivia's arm and guided her unsteadily to the prostrate idol. Greased hands and arms snaked around and mauled her legs and breasts and face and hair. She swooned and shuddered as the hands lifted her. She protested not as they carried and positioned her above the vertical and waiting phallus. Her legs were eased open. Disembodied fingers pinched and prodded and poked. She stared down with wide eyes and hot pink cheeks. Her hair, glossed with ointment and perspiration, stuck to her forehead, throat and shoulders. Her breasts and thighs glistened. "Please ..." she looked at the Abbess and whimpered, but even Olivia didn't know whether it was a plea for mercy or a request to be lowered and filled.

The Abbess stared deeply with amber eyes, searching Olivia's very soul, and then nodded. Hands on her shoulders bore gently down. The tip of the unmoving phallus nudged Olivia's labia.

"Ahhh ... it's too big!" she breathed.

"Wine," ordered the Abbess. "Give her some wine."

Sister Lupa instantly fetched a jug and raised the lip for Olivia to drink. She swallowed greedily and the rich red liquid spilled out over her chest. It trickled down between her breasts, over her ribs and stomach, and around her tummy-button to her pubes. The warm liquid relaxed her further. Hands forced her further down the slippery column.

"I can't do it!" she wailed, more out of frustrated disappointment than trepidation.

"You can," urged the Abbess

Olivia caught her breath and froze. The downward pressure increased. She relaxed as much as possible, and then to her immense relief and delight her buttocks settled down on the cold thighs. Olivia swayed dreamily with the marble penis buried deep inside her wonderfully stretched vagina. "I'm finished," she sobbed. Reaching forward blindly she clutched the rising breasts to steady herself. The nipples prodded into her palms. She remained thus for several uninterrupted minutes, gasping and groaning.

Olivia opened her eyes and through salty tears saw the Abbess sitting on the face of the idol. Her red dress was also tied up around her waist and off her shoulders to reveal her delicious breasts. She seductively ground her hips and writhed on the marble features whilst staring at Olivia the whole time. Her erect nipples pointed invitingly at Olivia, and she longed to feel them in her mouth.

The Abbess leaned forward and embraced her tightly. Their greased breasts swayed and caressed together.

Unseen by Olivia the Mistress gathered the whip and

awaited the signal. She was caught off guard. The thongs cut across her buttocks. Her shriek of shock and pain was smothered by the long kiss from the Abbess.

"Do not fight it, Olivia Holland," she panted and held the impaled girl tighter. "Concentrate on the energy inside you. The whip is only to enhance the pleasure. Watch me." The whip lashed into her own bottom. The soft flesh lifted slightly off the enigmatic face. Her expression clearly reflected the undiluted ecstasy coursing through her body. The amber eyes flashed from both pain and pleasure.

At that moment Olivia knew beyond doubt. She was here. The exquisite vision that had floated down from the heavens of the infirmary ceiling to make beautiful love to her was here now - holding her.

The whip fell again, but Olivia no longer felt the scorching pain. She gazed through a cloud of pleasure at the mass of nuns. They danced and gyrated. Wine was flowing and the flute and drum were increasing in tempo. Whips slashed and buttocks quivered. Some of the nuns now wore large penises strapped around their hips. They were making love like men. Olivia spied Flora, who was plunging just such a penis into poor Sister Alysoun. The girl was on her back and Flora bucked and stabbed between her legs, but despite her recent punishment Sister Alysoun clutched feverishly at her lover's buttocks and urged her to greater efforts. She whispered encouragement and winced with obvious delight as Flora set up a frantic pace.

Warm lips fastened onto Olivia's nipples and brought her back to the Abbess. She ran her fingers through the lustrous auburn hair and held the Abbess close to her breast. Fingers searched between her thighs and found her clitoris. Olivia's passions overwhelmed her. The whip fell again and again. Olivia rose to meet it. The column stretched her and the fingers strummed her erect bud. She could resist no longer. With a loud whimper she buried her face in the sweet-smelling hair and erupted into orgasm. Her whole body shuddered, and then she fell limp, breathing deeply.

The Abbess kissed her affectionately. "Stay as you are for a while, Sister Olivia. Allow the pleasures to sooth your mind and body."

"Sister Olivia?" she sighed. "Is it all over?"

"Almost. You have done well. I always knew you were special, Olivia."

"Was it necessary to have me flogged?"

"Pain before pleasure," the Abbess reminded her.

"Spiritus Licentia Copulatum," Olivia murmured dreamily. She looked around at the tableau of satiated bodies. The air was thick with sweat and heady feminine odour. Incense still drifted from the tripods.

As Flora and Sister Lupa helped the Abbess down from the altar the congregation slowly stirred and drifted into a fairly loose line. One by one they approached the rail, knelt and drank from a chalice held by the Mistress. Flora and Sister Lupa returned and lifted Olivia from the column of marble. Her limbs ached and she flinched as her stiff legs straightened and gingerly took the weight. Once the last nun had taken a sip from the chalice and returned down the aisle Olivia was helped forward. She knelt and drank. The refreshing liquid tasted faintly of mint and poppy seed. It cleared her head well.

Olivia stood. Rather appropriately the white gown loosened around her hips and rustled down to cover her legs once again. Flora lifted it back into place on her shoulders and hid her breasts. She then led her to the alcove where Sister Lupa had taken her during the ceremony.

As Olivia watched a nun entered through the chapel doors. She was fully clothed in a habit, and with head bowed made her way directly up the aisle to the Mistress.

She knelt, and as she looked up and raised her hands for the chalice Olivia realized she had never previously noticed her around the convent. She also noticed she was a little older than her sisters; still extremely attractive, but perhaps in her early thirties.

"Who is she?" Olivia asked of Flora, but before the reply came the truth struck her like a thunderbolt. Her earlier questions were just about to be answered. This nun was indeed older than the others, and Olivia had the distinct impression she was preparing to leave the order.

"Where did she come from?" she asked. "I don't recognize her."

"You won't," whispered Flora. "She's been kept in solitary confinement since your arrival here."

"But why? What's she done wrong?"

"She's done nothing wrong."

"So what will happen to her?"

Flora smiled. "You are her replacement, Olivia. It is her time to retire from the order."

"Retire?"

"She must go now and help provide earnings for the convent."

"And how will she do that?"

Flora smiled again. "You have much to learn Olivia. You are so naïve."

Suddenly the truth dawned. "You mean ... she's going to sell her body?"

"Yes - I do mean that."

Olivia couldn't believe what she was hearing. She watched the nun rise and the Mistress kiss both her cheeks as the meaning of Flora's words sank in. "But - but I haven't seen any men visiting the convent," she stammered.

Flora chuckled. "Of course you haven't. The entrance to that part of the building is not through the gate, but through an outer door which is always locked."

So that was it! Once each nun was considered too old for the order they were despatched to an internal brothel to help finance the upkeep of the convent, thereby making room for the next young innocent to stumble into the web and take her place.

There were a hundred questions rattling around in Olivia's head, but as she opened her mouth to utter the first of them the Abbess looked at Flora and then turned to leave the chapel. "Go to her quarters, Olivia," said Flora. "Tonight you belong to the Abbess. Be sure to please her well."

CHAPTER TWENTY ONE

Olivia took up the knife and chopped at the herbs Sister Lupa had laid out for her. She went about her task without thinking, like a skivvy going through her daily routine whilst dreaming of a handsome prince who would one day whisk her off to paradise. She chopped the herbs and put them in a bowl, then fetched a basket and tipped the contents onto the bench. Outside, the first snows of winter were falling from the heavy grey skies, clinging to the walls and turning the paths to a muddy slush.

"Mushrooms," said Sister Lupa, placing another basket on the bench. "Special mushrooms - the favourite of the Abbess. See to them, and I'll be back in a short while."

Olivia peered wearily at the basket's contents, and then set about slicing and adding them to the bowl of herbs. She had taken Flora's advice and apprenticed herself to the herbalist. It had taken a while to get accustomed to the stifling heat and the stench in the herbarium, but now she was able to close her mind to the tedium and get on with her chores without complaint. She did her best to convey a conscientious attitude, and everybody - including the suspicious Mistress - seemed pleased with her conformist attitude and efforts.

Once all the mushrooms had been sliced she filled the bowl with boiling water. On top of that she sprinkled dried rosemary and left it to ferment. While the concoction stewed she went out into the alleyway behind the herbarium for some clean fresh air. There was nobody about. The low thick cloud intensified the enveloping silence. The snow felt deliciously refreshing as she scooped it up and dabbed it on her grimy face. She allowed it to melt and slither down her front. Her thin working tunic soon became wet and clung to her breasts, her cold nipples clearly erect within. She so loved the pure crispness of the white snow she couldn't resist taking a handful and actually slipping it inside her tunic to rub it around her firm bosom. It melted on contact with her hot skin. She rubbed it over her nipples, shivering as they throbbed and tingled. Looking around to be sure she was alone, she lifted the skirt and rubbed some more of the freezing snow into her bottom. It felt very good. She flicked her nipples between finger and thumb and pressed between her buttocks to the secret opening. Her eyes closed.

"Why not let me do that?"

Olivia squealed and jumped at the untimely interruption.

Sister Lupa scooped some virgin snow from the top of a low wall and moved close to her delicious assistant. She embraced her and cupped her buttocks. Icy water trickled down the back of Olivia's thighs and tickled the back of her knees. One hand delved into the same warm valley that Olivia had herself just been probing, and the other burrowed between her thighs and sought her clitoris without hesitation. Olivia couldn't suppress a groan of delight at the twin assault. She squirmed and squashed her wet and aching breasts against Sister Lupa's.

"You're coming along very nicely, Sister Olivia," the herbalist panted in her ear. "You're the most promising assistant I've ever been permitted to work upon."

"Thank you," sighed Olivia as one digit prodded delicately just inside her rear passage. "I - I try to do my best."

A vibrant tongue wormed into her mouth, and she ground herself on the fingers which slipped back and forth in her wet vagina. Sister Lupa was as gentle as usual, and Olivia always encouraged her to be as intimate as she liked. Besides the fact that she genuinely enjoyed their times together and the experimenting with oils and aphrodisiacs, she also knew that reports on her progress were going back to the Abbess and the Mistress, and that it was important to build on the confidence she had already instilled in them. As they relaxed and gradually watched her less and less she was able to learn something of the geography of the convent; its labyrinthine passages and cellars, workshops and halls. A plan was forming in her mind, and now was the time to carefully test its likelihood of success. As Sister Lupa nibbled and kissed Olivia's ear she herself looked over the herbalist's shoulder at the low door at the end of the cobbled alleyway. Behind it, Olivia knew, the older nuns lived out their lives, servicing the traders who delivered to the convent and any other gentlemen who wished to come and pay for their pleasures. The door was only used by the nuns who took them their provisions. The customers entered and exited through a discreet door in the castle wall. That was the door that led to freedom.

"Shall we?" Sister Lupa panted as she backed Olivia

towards the grey wall.

"Shall we what?"

"Make love, here in the snow."

Olivia knew the herbalist was highly excited. "But we'll freeze to death," she teased.

Sister Lupa kept guiding Olivia backwards until they were beneath an arch and out of the falling white flakes. When Olivia leaned back against the wall she was surprised to find it pleasantly warm.

"It's the fire in the herbarium," Sister Lupa told her. "We're right behind it. You've no excuse about freezing now," she smiled.

"You've been here before."

The two of them kissed deeply. Olivia squeezed Sister Lupa's bottom and pulled her as close as possible. The finger sank further into her own bottom. "I want you to fuck me," she panted.

Sister Lupa groaned at the tantalizing thought.

"Please ..." whimpered Olivia in her sexiest voice. "Please fetch your dildo. I want you to do it right here - right now."

Sister Lupa needed no further encouragement. She kissed Olivia, looked at her longingly, and then hastily scurried away to her quarters.

By the time she returned the alleyway was empty. Olivia was not awaiting her return beneath the arch. There were many fairly fresh footprints, gradually filling with snow, and there was a small bloodstain slowly disappearing beneath the white blanket. What had happened? Olivia must have slipped on some ice, causing an abrasion, and taken herself to the infirmary. The extra footprints must have been a passing nun who had stopped to offer assistance. Sister Lupa's passion was ebbing in the cold.

Never mind, she would keep it simmering in the herbarium and await Olivia's return.

"I'm sorry about the Sister," apologized Olivia as sincerely as she could. Her heart pounded as the low door locked behind her and the two other nuns bearing baskets of bread.

"I said forget it," snapped a burly nun with a mole on her chin. "She'll be all right once she gets her knee cleaned up."

"I don't know how she tripped over my foot like that."

"Be quiet," hissed the second nun. "If you're found in here we'll all be in very big trouble."

"But I'm only trying to help - how else would you have coped with three large baskets such as these?"

"I said be quiet!"

Olivia fell silent and followed a short distance at their heels, careful not to betray any excitement or to anger them further by saying any more.

"Quick, in here," directed the nun with the mole. "Put the bread on the table. And be quick about it."

The second nun set about emptying the baskets in what appeared to be a pantry of some sort. The nun with the mole steered Olivia back out to the passage and towards the door. "Now get out," she snapped. "And quickly!"

Olivia turned the huge iron key in the door, opened it, checked over her shoulder that the nun had disappeared back into the pantry, and slammed the door shut. It was the biggest gamble she'd taken in her whole life. She peeped around the corner. The nuns were talking to each other and sorting the loaves. Unseen, Olivia stole like a shadow up a nearby flight of stairs. Like a thief she flitted along a narrow landing, not knowing where she was going or how she would ever reach the outer door. Her head span and her heart thumped so loudly in her chest she was convinced someone would hear it and catch her before she made good her escape. She had to be quick. As soon as the two nuns went back out to the cobbled alleyway Sister Lupa would surely be waiting, and then all of hell would break loose.

Her pulse quickened when she peered out of a grimy window. She was on the first floor overlooking the black icy road that wound away from the castle through the white fields. She could see below what she assumed was the door to freedom. It was so close she could have wept. How to reach it? So desperate was she to get away she even contemplated the risk of breaking her back by jumping from the window, and might have done so had a voice not spun her around.

"And what are you doing here?"

"I - I'm lost," she blurted absurdly.

The nun shook her head knowingly and ordered her up another flight of steps and into her room. A fire crackled in the grate.

"Stand still by the table," was the first thing she said to the startled Olivia once she had bolted the door.

"Please don't punish me -" Olivia begged. "I don't mean any harm. I'll do anything you ask - just please don't tell the Abbess you found me here. I'll be in enough trouble as it is; Sister Lupa will surely be wondering where I am."

The nun made no response as she closed the shutters on her window and lit a candle. In the dim glow and the dancing light from the fire she studied her beautiful visitor from the corner of her eye. Her face bore no expression.

"If you do exactly as you're told," she eventually said quietly, "I can get you back into the convent without anyone ever knowing you were here." She looked long and hard at Olivia. "That is, of course, assuming you want to go back to the convent."

Olivia didn't know whether to trust her or not. "Of course

I do."

They stared at each other; waging a mental war. The nun sat beside the fire.

"You do not wish to escape then, Olivia Holland?"

"How do you know my name?" Olivia stammered.

"Never you mind." The nun spoke smoothly and confidently. "Do you not wish to escape from here?"

Olivia studied the enigmatic nun closely. She was extremely attractive and retained a shapely figure, that much was apparent despite the plain habit.

"If you do wish to escape," she continued, "then I can help."

"And why would you do that?" asked Olivia carefully.

"Because I too must escape. Because I cannot take another week of whoring myself in this hell-hole simply to increase the wealth of the greatest whores of them all - the Abbess and the Mistress!" Anger suddenly raged in her eyes and she spat the words as if she hated their very presence in her mouth. She looked into the fire and calmed herself for a few long minutes.

Olivia still didn't know whether to trust her. This could easily be another trick being played by the Abbess or the Mistress. "Then why do you not escape, if you hate it here so much?"

"Olivia," the nun smiled sadly and looked around the tiny room. "I have been living - if one can use that word - living in this place for sixteen years now. When I was lured here I was nothing more than a naïve teenager. I know not the ways of the outside world, and would survive no more than five minutes out there."

Olivia looked a little quizzical. "And what has this to do with me?"

"I will help you escape, but in return you must promise to stay with me for an agreed time. You must teach me how to survive until I can find my family."

"But what makes you think I can help you do that? If I was that clever I would not be here in the first place."

"You will be better equipped to cope for your experiences here."

Olivia suspected that was true.

"Besides," the nun was still talking, "I have been keeping a watchful eye on your progress since your arrival here -"

"How have you done that, locked up in this depressing place the whole time?"

"We have our ways and means. And I know you are a young woman of great potential." The nun leaned forward with hope flashing in her eyes. "Olivia, together we can do well outside!"

"But I failed to get away with Walpurga. Perhaps I'd do better on my own."

"Walpurga is stupid!" the nun hissed. "And don't forget - you need me just as much as I need you."

Olivia was beginning to suspect that was also true. Her head was in a spin. What should she do? This woman was a complete stranger - but she was the first stranger she'd met since this nightmare began who hadn't instantly taken advantage of her misfortune. It could be highly risky, but then wasn't she in this part of the castle for the very reason of escaping? Being here was in itself a risk. Having come this far there was no going back. She looked at the nun; she had no intention of sitting here in sixteen years and begging for help like her. "What's your name?" she asked after a long pause.

"Vita," answered the nun without hesitating.

"Very well, Vita - I will help you, and we will leave here together."

Vita visibly relaxed and smiled broadly. She cuddled Olivia and kissed her cheek, but it was a cuddle and a kiss of genuine affection rather than sexual intent. "Come," she said, "we must make haste!"

Quickly they made their way through another maze of passages. Vita explained that all the nuns were taking their afternoon nap before the rigours of the nightshift began, so there was little chance of discovery. At the bottom of a long long flight of dark stone steps they came to a tiny oak door. Vita slipped the bolt and ushered Olivia through.

"You're in the crypt beneath the chapel," she whispered. She told Olivia to meet her there the following evening after chapel, and closed and locked the door. Olivia was in silent cold darkness. She hastily scrambled her way out of the macabre place, and made her way back to the herbarium.

"And where have you been, young lady?" snapped the Mistress.

Olivia was shocked to find her waiting with Sister Lupa. This could mean big trouble and a quick end to her plan for escape with Vita. "I - um - I fell over, and went back to my cell to wash the wound." She cringed at the feeble excuse; they would next ask to see the scraped knee.

"Really?" said the Mistress without conviction. "What do you think Sister Lupa?"

Sister Lupa gazed upon Olivia's lovely breasts and nipples still clearly visible through the damp material, and her previously aroused passions continued to simmer. She wanted the Mistress to leave as quickly as possible. "I did see some blood outside in the snow," she said. "And Sister Olivia has always been extremely honest and diligent in her duties here."

"Has she indeed?"

Olivia was just waiting for the dreaded order to raise the hem of her tunic.

"Well … let's just see how honest she is, shall we?" Olivia squealed as the Mistress grabbed her arm and dragged her over to the workbench. "Birch!" she snapped to Sister Lupa.

"Oh, no!" cried Olivia, more from the realization that her tunic would be raised to the waist than the fear of the implement.

"Oh yes! Wet it!"

Sister Lupa dipped the twigs into a bucket of water and handed them to the mistress.

"Over the bench! Hold her arms still, Sister Lupa!"

Olivia obeyed fearfully, and immediately felt her wrists pinned to the wooden surface. A claw-like hand smoothed over her bottom. She held her breath. Any moment now and the material would slide up and expose her unblemished legs. The fingers probed and pushed the material between her buttocks. They left her, and then a vicious swish was followed by a searing pain through her raised cheeks. She bucked against the bench and grit her teeth.

"Let us see how honest you are!" panted the Mistress.

Another swish and the hands struggled to keep a grip on Olivia's jerking wrists. She would not scream for mercy!

"Where have you been?!"

"In my cell!"

"What were you doing there?!" The birch cut down again and a little of it splintered away under the force of the impact.

"Attending to my knee!"

Another blow swept into her poor bottom and she bit her lip. The Mistress stopped the punishment and stood panting heavily. The hand returned and smoothed the tunic over Olivia's blazing flesh - almost tenderly. Olivia relaxed a little. "Very well …" said the Mistress softly, "I believe you … But this is for not being where you were supposed to be!" and the birch whistled through the air and caught Olivia an excruciating blow at the top of her thighs. She reared up. Her breasts lifted off the bench and swelled as she inhaled deeply, but it didn't look as if her lie would be discovered, and the consolation that she would soon be away from the cruel bespectacled bitch helped her through the pain.

"Now get yourself cleaned up and back to your work," ordered the Mistress as she threw the implement onto the bench and stormed from the herbarium.

Olivia straightened up and carefully rubbed her sore bottom. Sister Lupa watched with some sympathy in her eyes. Olivia knew she had to consolidate her total trust and allay any suspicions which may be lingering there. "Why don't you soothe me with some of your oils, Lupa," she whispered as sweetly as she knew how. "I'd like that. You're so good at it."

"Very well," she said. "Bend over the bench again and lift your skirts ... I have something very special to take your mind off the pain."

Olivia decided Sister Lupa's mind was on things other than whether she had a grazed knee or not. She bent over once again, lifted her tunic as slowly and seductively as possible, leant on her elbows, and pouted over her shoulder.

Sister Lupa almost fell over not one but two stools in her haste to retrieve a sealed jar from one of her shelves. She then went to her desk and took something which Olivia could not quite see; the afternoon was closing in and the herbarium growing quite gloomy. She returned to be presented with the breathtaking sight of Olivia's bared bottom and her light covering of curly down peeping from her slightly parted thighs. The vivid red weals ran horizontally across each cheek, and she silently cursed the Mistress for damaging such a priceless specimen.

"Keep still, my darling," she whispered, and caressed a little of the secret oil into Olivia's soft flesh. The pain somehow disappeared instantly, and Olivia wriggled her hips to encourage the clever herbalist to proceed further. Sister Lupa's fingers pressed more firmly into the glossy and slippery twin-cheeks. She allowed them to stray between Olivia's already wet labia. Her patient sighed and twisted her hips again. "Just a moment," she whispered. "I have something else for you - a special treat."

She lifted her own tunic, took the phallus from where it hid in the deep pocket, and strapped it around her hips.

"What are you doing, Lupa?" Olivia pleaded softly, as if she didn't really know.

"Just a moment ... stay as you are." She dipped her fingers once again into the jar and then coated the phallus which sprouted from her groin. Her fist slipped easily up and down its formidable length and girth. "Now then my darling, open your legs just a little wider."

Sister Lupa shuffled forward between Olivia's spread feet. She positioned the lubricated dome at Olivia's wet entrance and gripped her hips. "Are you ready?" she asked.

Olivia rested her forehead on the bench and nodded.

Sister Lupa's buttocks hollowed and her breasts swayed as she lunged forward and sank relentlessly into her arching and groaning patient.

Olivia closed her eyes and smiled contentedly as she leaned all the way back against the herbalist and felt hands cup and squeeze her breasts through the tunic. She would soon be free, and in the meantime she would enjoy being seduced by the handsome nun whose trust in her had proved so critical.

CHAPTER TWENTY TWO

The bolt clunked and Olivia tumbled through the tiny oak door and into Vita's arms.

"Olivia - what have they done to you?" Vita asked with genuine concern.

Olivia smiled. "Don't worry. The Mistress decided to beat me for being absent without permission, and then Sister Lupa very kindly gave me a going away present."

Vita looked shocked. "She knows?"

"No, of course not," Olivia reassured, and then added with a glint in her eye: "But she soon will."

"Are you able enough to do what needs to be done this night?"

"What do you think, Vita? Nothing will stand between us and freedom."

They were back in the safe warmth of Vita's room. She wore nothing more than a nightgown. Muffled sounds from through the walls suggested that other nuns were stirring in readiness to receive their male customers.

"What now?" asked Olivia.

"We have a little while to wait. I have arranged for a customer to visit us."

"Why?" Olivia was shocked.

"You'll see soon enough." It was Vita's turn to reassure. "Be still - he is a good man. A little simple - but a good man."

She went to the window and peered through the shutters.

Night had fallen. "Let us prepare as much as we are able," she said, going to her only cabinet.

She moved it a few feet with her shoulder, stopped to make sure the noise had not alerted anyone, and then dropped onto all fours and lifted a couple of loose floorboards. Olivia watched agog as a bundle and a pair of boots were retrieved from the secret hiding-place and tossed onto the bed.

"Get dressed," Vita told her as she unwrapped the bundle and handed her a shirt and a pair of breeches. There was also a coat which she laid on the table. Olivia loved the excitement, and hastily tore off her habit. She slipped into the breeches and picked up the shirt.

"Just a minute," said Vita, ripping a strip off her bed-sheet. "Wrap this tightly around your bosom." She looked at the topless beauty. It seemed such a shame to cover them, but there would be plenty of time to appreciate her attributes later. As she opened the door slightly and peered down the landing Olivia bound herself - with some difficulty, such were her generous proportions - and completed her costume. The boots were old and far too large, but she slipped her feet into them nonetheless.

"I'm ready," she beamed.

Vita turned and smiled at her. "Not quite - put your hair up," and she took a wide-brimmed hat from the bundle and planted it firmly atop Olivia's adorable head. "Now you are ready," she announced with satisfaction. She checked the shirt and the breeches. "A little oversized," she decided, "but they'll do until we can find something more suitable."

"What will you wear?" asked Olivia, but before Vita could answer there started from the next room the churning of bedsprings and harsh grunts. "The customers are arriving - he'll be here soon."

At that precise moment there was a quiet tap on the door. Vita opened it quickly and a man slipped into the room. He wasn't a large man, about the same size as Vita, and Olivia didn't quite like the look of him. He was dressed in a similar fashion to herself, complete with floppy hat. As Vita checked the landing again and closed the door the man spied Olivia, sucked his one tooth, and scratched the stubble on his chin. If this was her best customer, Olivia couldn't imagine what her worst must be like!

"So ..." the man said to Vita whilst studying Olivia from head to toe and back to head. "You still be leavin' us tonight."

"Of course."

"Is this be the one who's goin' wiv you?"

"Yes Barnaby - this is Olivia," answered Vita ... a little anxiously, Olivia noticed curiously. She decided the imminent escape must be making her nervous.

Barnaby scratched his stubble all the more and stepped close to Olivia. "Take yer 'at off," he said suddenly. Olivia looked to Vita and saw in her eyes that for some reason she must obey. She removed the hat and her glorious black hair tumbled back down around her shoulders. He squinted at her, and suddenly reached out and gripped where her breasts were strapped and hidden beneath the capacious shirt.

"Oh," Olivia squealed, a little taken aback by this unexpected move. She stood still and allowed him to assess her restricted contours, although she wasn't sure why she did allow him such a liberty.

"Right," Barnaby eventually said over his shoulder. "She do."

Vita looked greatly relieved. Olivia suspected something was afoot. "What's going on, Vita?"

"Barnaby has heard all about you," Vita shuffled

uncomfortably. "He'll help us escape ... but he wants something in return."

"And what might that something be?" asked Olivia, expecting the worst.

"You. He wants you."

"No Vita," Olivia shook her head.

"But you must - he's our only chance."

"We must go now," urged Olivia, "before we're all discovered."

"We have time," Vita argued. "It would be best to wait until later - to wait until most of the castle is asleep."

Olivia sighed. She knew she had little choice at this late stage. And she still desperately wanted to escape. "You should have told me the whole deal Vita. This isn't fair."

Vita looked a little sheepish. "I'm sorry Olivia. I didn't know what to do."

"Why did you have me dress in these clothes," she asked, "if you knew I would just as quickly have to take them off again?"

"Just in case something went wrong and we had to make a hasty exit."

Olivia was beginning to wish something had gone wrong. She placed the hat on the table, sat on the bed, and began to unbutton her shirt. She looked up at the man, who stood watching her hungrily but without moving. "Are you not going to make yourself a little more comfortable, Barnaby?" she said as pleasantly as she could.

He started to open his breeches and kicked off his boots. "Aye. But me coat, an' shirt, an' me 'at stays on - until I'se bin paid."

As soon as he was naked from the waist down he approached Olivia and pushed her down onto the bed by her shoulders. She was still fully clothed, but he didn't seem to mind about that. Vita sat on the bed and cuddled

Olivia's head in her lap. 'Thank you', she mouthed silently to Olivia, and loosened the remainder of her shirt buttons.

Barnaby undid Olivia's breeches and tugged them down, but in his haste to enjoy this rather special morsel he only bothered to get them down to her knees. She had no underwear on, which was useful and afforded him instant access. He tugged her legs apart as far as the breeches would allow, and then fumbled crudely between her thighs. Despite her apprehension, Olivia felt her juices quickly anoint his fingers. Her nipples strained painfully against the tight strip of sheeting.

Vita gently lay the shirt open, and Barnaby instantly swooped and bit and kissed Olivia's exposed throat. "Vita!" he croaked into the soft flesh, "get me in 'er. I wants 'er now!"

Vita squeezed her hand between the two bodies and found his cock. It was stabbing into Olivia's thighs and belly. She milked it with a few firm strokes, trying to bring him closer to his climax and thereby bringing Olivia's ordeal to a hastier conclusion. His buttocks clenched and his hips jerked instinctively.

"Don't cheat me Vita!" he warned from between Olivia's cleavage which bulged from the strapping. "I'se wants my part o' the deal ... now!"

Vita looked again at Olivia, and held her imploring stare as she positioned the engorged helmet at her entrance, and then fed the stalk into her. Olivia inhaled deeply as the flesh sank deeper and deeper, and Barnaby took advantage of this to bury his nose even further into her spectacular cleavage. Vita's hand became wedged between soft pubic hair on one side and coarse pubic hair on the other. With her free hand she stroked Olivia's damp hair away from her forehead. She knew that because of the restrictive breeches Barnaby would feel abnormally large inside her.

She watched Olivia groan and jerk on the mattress as Barnaby began to buck against her. The whole bed shook and banged against the wall.

Suddenly Barnaby held himself up on straightened arms and leered down at his prize. "I'se goin' to come now," he gloated. He looked at Vita with bulging eyes. "It be true - she's bloody good! Now you open yer gown too," he ordered. Vita obeyed and bared her breasts. Her nipples were already erect from the stimulation of holding Olivia and watching while she was taken by the man.

Olivia looked from him to Vita, and then closed her eyes and waited. She was unmoved by the cold coupling, but still her muscles instinctively caressed the pulsing column within.

Barnaby latched onto one of Vita's nipples and sucked it deep. He thrust his hips rapidly a number of times and then stiffened, pumping his seed into Olivia's vagina. He thrust a few more times, released another load into her, and then rolled away and lay on the bed grinning up at the ceiling like a village idiot. His glistening cock stood up twitching, and dribbled a combination of juices onto his shirt.

The three of them remained quiet and still for a while, each with their own thoughts. Eventually Vita rose and removed her gown altogether.

"Come on then Barnaby," she said. "Give me your clothes. It's time we were going."

As she bound her own breasts and dressed in his clothes Olivia rose without a sound, straightened her own outfit, and put on the coat. Soon they were both ready.

"Haven't you forgotten something?" Vita asked.

Barnaby grinned. "It's in me coat pocket."

Vita delved deep and retrieved what she was looking for; a large iron key.

Olivia could now almost laugh at the sight of Barnaby's skinny frame and his sleeping penis hanging uselessly between his bandy legs. He wore nothing more than a pair of dirty socks through which poked his big toes.

"Make it look convincin', Vita," he grinned.

Vita looked at him with a glint in her eye. "Oh, I will Barnaby … I will." She ripped another strip off the rapidly diminishing sheet and tied his wrists to the bed frame. "Convincing, you say?"

Barnaby sat on the bed. "Aye. I don't want the Abbess or the Mistress suspectin' an' stoppin' me from ever comin' 'ere again - now do I?"

"No Barnaby - I don't suppose you do." She picked up the clay water jug, and then handed it to Olivia. "Would you?"

Barnaby's grin quickly evaporated when he saw the look in Olivia's eyes. He tried to protest but the jug shattered over his head before one syllable could be uttered. Water soaked him and he slumped back against the wall, cracking his head a second time and ensuring him a good night's sleep.

"Thank you," said Olivia with a satisfied smile and a straightening of her coat lapels.

The two of them put on their hats, and slipped out onto the dark landing. Vita clutched the iron key as though their lives depended on it - which they quite possibly did.

CHAPTER TWENTY THREE

Olivia's heart leapt. At the end of the passage was the outer door, and to the right of it a room whose own door was closed. Let into this door was a small grill. The light from it sent an orange glow into the passage. Vita peeped carefully through, and then turned back ashen-faced. Olivia squeezed her legs together, wishing she had used the pot before they set out. They were so close now, the tension was almost too much to bear.

"You have been rude and disobedient," a man's voice said firmly from within the room. "And now I have to punish you. Bend over."

"Please, no ... Spare me."

Olivia stared at Vita with wide disbelieving eyes. She could hardly believe her ears.

"You need discipline," the male voice continued. "Take off your clothes - immediately!"

A whip or cane landed with a dull smack followed by a shriek. Clothes rustled off and a hoarse laugh came through the grill. Olivia recognized the voice begging for mercy instantly. She joined Vita and squinted into the room.

"A dozen at least," the man said joyfully, swishing the implement again over the bare haunches of the bespectacled Mistress.

Olivia and Vita drew back into the shadows. They couldn't risk opening the outer door yet; the Mistress would expect an arriving or departing customer, and they couldn't risk being recognized by her. "What now?" Olivia whispered, still shocked at the sight of the Mistress hiring herself out for a caning.

Vita shrugged and whispered back: "We wait."

They stood like naughty schoolgirls outside a governor's office, listening to the smack of cane on flesh, awaiting their own punishment. Olivia couldn't resist seeing what was going on inside. Neither could Vita. They peered around each corner of the grill and breathed as quietly as humanly possible.

"No!" shrieked the Mistress, tearing at the bonds which tied her wrists to the back of a chair. An expensive cigar smouldered in a nearby ashtray. A velvet frock-coat draped over a desk, half covering a ledger. Beside it was a pocketbook stuffed with notes. Whoever was beating her was very rich. The Mistress obviously had no intentions of retiring in the convent brothel.

"Keep still!" the stranger roared. His impatience sounded genuine.

The open legs of the Mistress went rigid as the cane slashed into her bottom. She let out a muffled cry and started sobbing. He hit her thighs and she screamed with agony. A dozen or so more strokes fell on her buttocks sending her into wild spasms. The man half-turned and the girls ducked from sight.

When they ventured to spy again his trousers were precisely folded atop his frock-coat and his shirt-tails were tucked around his rotund paunch. He seized his plaything's hips and pulled her backwards onto his unimpressive erection with no further ado.

"This wasn't in the bargain!" the Mistress complained.

"Be quiet and keep still," came the reply, accentuated with a cuff around the back of the head.

The girls watched in disbelief as the stranger sank into the Mistress until his groin nestled against her rump and his paunch rested on her buttocks. The Mistress grunted and gripped the chair, knuckles turning white as he commenced riding her.

"A splendid piece of work," he complimented, slapping her flanks.

The Mistress muttered something incomprehensible and tugged at the ropes again. He slapped her flank and pulled back to the edge of her labia. Another slap and he filled her with a single plunge. To the sounds of flesh striking flesh and the Mistress squealing like a stuck pig Olivia turned away and clamped a hand over her mouth to suppress the giggle which threatened to give them away.

"Now for your mouth!" she heard, and then Vita joined her and together they smothered each other's laughter.

"No! You filthy …!"

After a few minutes of mumbled curses and wet sucking sounds they heard the man grunt abruptly. There was another quiet spell when only heavy breathing could be heard, and then the man spoke in a considerably more genial tone. "Five guineas I believe you said."

"Yes sir - thank you sir," Olivia and Vita heard a very humble Mistress reply. There was a swish of expensive sounding material, and then the man came out of the room wearing his frock-coat and top hat and carrying his gold-topped cane. "I'll let myself out," he called over his shoulder.

Olivia and Vita pulled their hats down over their eyes and stood in the shadows as if they had just arrived there and were about to leave the brothel also.

"Just leaving, gentlemen?" the man asked conveniently.

They both nodded. Vita held up her key but the man had already inserted his in the lock. Olivia trembled with excitement. There was a blast of cold air and a little flurry of snow as the outer door finally opened.

"You appear to have no form of transport gentleman," said the man as he locked the door from the outside; too slowly for Olivia's liking. "Would you care for a lift somewhere?"

Olivia and Vita shook their heads and kept their brims low.

"Suit yourselves," the man said, and crunched across the snow to his waiting carriage without another word.

As the vehicle slithered and rattled its way out onto the icy highway Olivia and Vita clung to the rear luggage rack. Their hands burned from the cold as they clung on and the biting wind froze their faces, but their eyes and their broad grins sparkled in the crisp moonlit night. Inviting orange lights from a town or village twinkled in the distance.

Olivia looked back, but they were already into another valley and the terrible castle was out of sight and out of her life forever. Now she could only consider the road ahead - wherever that may lead ...

Already available from Chimera:

1-901388-20-4 The Instruction of Olivia *Allen*
1-901388-05-0 Flame of Revenge *Scott*
1-901388-10-7 The Switch *Keir*
1-901388-15-8 Captivation *Fisher*
1-901388-00-X Sweet Punishment *Jameson*
1-901388-25-5 Afghan Bound *Morgan*

Coming soon from Chimera:

1-901388-02-6 Belinda: Cruel Passage West *Caine (Sept '97)*
1-901388-03-4 Twilight in Berlin *Deutsch (Oct '97)*
1-901388-04-2 Thunder's Slaves *Leather (Nov '97)*
1-901388-06-9 Schooling Sylvia *Beaufort (Dec '97)*
1-901388-07-7 Under Orders *Asquith (Jan '98)*

All the above are/will be available at your local bookshop or newsagent, or by post or telephone from: B.B.C.S., P.O. Box 941, Hull, HU1 3VQ. **(24 hour Telephone Credit Card Line: 01482 224626)**.

To order, send: Title, author, ISBN number and price for each book ordered, your full name and address, cheque or postal order payable to B.B.C.S. for the total amount, and allow the following for postage and packing:
UK and BFPO: £1.00 for the first book, and 50p for each additional book to a maximum of £3.50.
Overseas and Eire: £2.00 for the first book, £1.00 for the second and 50p for each additional book.

All titles £4.99 (US$7.95*)

*Recommended Price